# PIMP FOR THE DEAD

## The Hardman Series

# PIMP FOR THE DEAD

RALPH DENNIS

BRASH
BOOKS

# INTRODUCTION

## Ralph Dennis and Hardman
## By Joe R. Lansdale

O nce upon the time there were a lot of original paperbacks, and like the pulps before them, they covered a lot of ground. Western, adventure, romance, mystery, science fiction, fantasy, and crime, for example.

There were also subsets of certain genres. One of those was the sexy, men's action-adventure novel with a dab of crime and mystery.

These books had suggestive titles, or indicators that not only were they action packed with blood and sweat, fists and bullets, but that there would be hot, wet sex. They were straight up from the male reader's perspective, the perspective of the nineteen seventies and early eighties.

There were entire lines of adult westerns for example. They sold well at the time. Quite well. These Westerns sold so well, that for a brief period it seemed as if it might go on forever. They made up the largest number of Westerns on the stands rivaled only by Louis L'Amour, and a few reprints from Max Brand and Zane Grey.

An agent once told me I was wasting my time writing other things, and I could be part of this big stable he had writing adult Westerns. Although I had nothing against sexy Westerns, which may in fact have been pioneered as a true branch of the Western genre by a very good writer named Brian Garfield and his novel *Sliphammer*, but I didn't want to spend a career writing them. Not the sort I had read, anyway.

Still, a small part of me, the part that was struggling to pay bills, thought maybe I could write something of that nature that might be good enough to put a pen name on. Many of my friends and peers were doing it, and some actually did it quite well, but if ever there was a formulaic brand of writing, that was it.

I was a big fan of Westerns in general, however, so I thought I might could satisfy that itch, while managing to satisfy the publisher's itch, not to mention that of the Adult Western reader, primarily males.

I picked up a number of the so called adult Westerns, read them, and even landed a job as a ghost for one series, but the publisher and the writer had a falling out, so my work was never published, though I got paid.

Actually, for me, that was the best-case scenario. Once I started on the series I knew I was in for trouble. It wasn't any fun for me, and that is the main reason I write. I woke up every morning feeling ill because I was trying to write that stuff. It was like trying to wear a tux to a tractor pull.

I thought, maybe there's something I would like more in the action-adventure line, crime, that sort of thing. I had read *The Executioner*, and had even written three in the *M.I.A. Hunter* series, and frankly, next to nailing my head to a burning building, I would rather have been doing anything else. But a look at our bank account made me more pliable.

But that was later. At the time I was looking at this sort of genre, trying to understand if there was anything in it I could truly like, I picked up a book by Ralph Dennis, *The Charleston Knife is Back in Town*, bearing the overall title of *Hardman*. The books were billed by the publisher as "a great new private eye for the shockproof seventies."

The title was suggestive in a non-subtle way, and I remember sighing, and cracking it open and hoping I could at least make it a third of the way through.

And then, it had me. It gripped me and carried me through, and one thing was immediately obvious. It wasn't a sex and shoot novel. It's not that those were not components, but not in the way of the other manufactured series, where sometimes the sex scenes were actually lifted from another one in the series and placed in the new one, in the perfunctory manner you might replace a typewriter ribbon.

I was working on a typewriter in those days, and so was everyone else. If that reference throws you, look it up. You'll find it somewhere between etched stone tablets and modern PCs.

Dennis wrote with assurance, and he built characterization through spot on first person narration. His prose was muscular, swift, and highly readable. There was an echo behind it.

Jim Hardman wasn't a sexy private eye with six-pack abs and face like Adonis. He was a pudgy, okay looking guy, and as a reader, you knew who Hardman was and how he saw things, including himself, in only a few pages.

You learned about him through dialogue and action. Dennis was good at both techniques. His action was swift and realistic, and you never felt as if something had been mailed in.

Hardman wasn't always likable, or good company. And he knew that about himself. He was a guy just trying to make it from day to day in a sweltering city. He had a friend named Hump, though Hardman was reluctant to describe him as such. In his view he and Hump were associates. He sometimes hired Hump to help him with cases where two men, and a bit of muscle, were needed.

That said, Hump was obviously important to Hardman, and as the series proceeded, he was more so. The books developed their world, that hot, sticky, Atlanta landscape, and it was also obvious that Dennis knew Atlanta well, or was at least able to give you the impression he did.

His relationship with Marcy, his girlfriend, had a convenient feel, more than that of a loving relationship, and it was off again and on again; it felt real, and the thing that struck me about the books was that there was real human fabric to them. There was action, of course, but like Chandler and Hammett before him, Dennis was trying to do something different with what was thought of as throw away literature.

I'm not suggesting Dennis was in the league of those writers, but he was certainly head and shoulders above the mass of paperbacks being put out fast and dirty. When I read Dennis's Hardman novels, the characters, the background, stayed with me. The stories were peripheral in a way. Like so many of the best modern crime stories, they were about character.

Due to the publishing vehicle and the purpose of the series, at least from the publisher's view point, the books sometimes showed a hastiness that undercut the best of the work, but, damn, I loved them. I snatched them up and devoured them.

I thought I might like to do something like that, but didn't, and a few years later I wrote those *M.I.A. Hunters*, which I actually loathed, and knew all my visitations with that branch of the genre I loved, crime and suspense, had ended, and not well, at least for me, though the three books were later collected and published in a hardback edition from Subterranean Press by me and its creator, Stephen Mertz.

A few years after that journey into the valley of death, quite a few, actually, I had a contract with Bantam, and I was trying to come up with a crime novel, and I wrote about this guy named Hap standing out in a field in East Texas, and with him, out of nowhere, was a gay, black guy named Leonard.

The idea of a black and white team in the depths of East Texas would be something I could write about, and it was a way for me to touch on social issues without having to make a parade of it. I thought, yeah, that'll work for me, and though my characters are quite different than Hardman, they share many similarities as well. The black and white team and Southern background (East Texas is more South than Southwestern), was certainly inspired by the Hardman novels. I think because it rang a bell with me, the clapper of that bell slapped up against my own personal experience, though mine was more rural than urban.

Even more than other writer heroes of mine, Chandler and Chester Himes for example, Hardman spoke directly to me. Chandler's language and wise cracks fit the people I grew up with, and Himes wrote about the black experience, something that was vital to the South, though often given a sideways consideration and the back of culture's hand. But Hardman had that white blue collar feel, even if he was in the city and was already an established, if unlicensed, private investigator and thug for hire. I blended all those writers, and many more, to make Hap and Leonard, John D. McDonald, certainly, but if I had a spirit guide with the Hap and Leonard books, it was Ralph Dennis.

So now we have the Hardman books coming back into print.

I am so excited about this neglected series being brought back, put in front of readers again. It meant a lot to me back then, and it still means a lot. You can beef about the deficiency of political correctness, but twenty years from now they'll be beefing about our lack of political correctness on some subject or another that we now think we are hip to. And too much political correctness is the enemy of truth, and certainly there are times when fiction is not about pretty manners but should ring the true bells of social conditions and expression. Erasing what is really going on, even in popular fiction, doesn't do anyone any favors. Righteous political correctness has its place, but political correct police do not.

I know very little about Ralph Dennis. I know this. He wrote other books outside the Hardman series. I don't think he had the career he deserved. The Hardman books were a product of their time, but they managed to be about their time, not of it. They stand head and shoulders above so much of the paperback fodder that was designed for men to hold the book in one hand, and something else in the other. And I don't mean a can of beer.

But one thing is for sure, these books are still entertaining, and they are a fine time capsule that addresses the nature and attitudes of the time in which they were written. They do that with clean, swift prose, sharp characterization, and an air of disappointment in humanity that seems more and more well-earned.

I'm certainly glad I picked that Hardman novel up those long years ago. They were just what I needed. An approach that imbedded in my brain like a knitting needle, mixed with a variety of other influences, and helped me find my own voice. An authentic Southern voice. A voice that wasn't that of New York or Los Angeles or Chicago, but a voice of the South.

Thanks Ralph Dennis for helping me recognize that my background was as good a fodder for popular fiction as any, and that popular fiction could attempt to rise above the common crime novel. I don't know that I managed that, but Ralph Dennis was one of those writers that made me try.

Dennis may not have made literature of Hardman, but he damn sure touched on it more than a time or two, and I wish you the joy I got from first reading these novels, so many long, years ago.

Read on.

# PUBLISHER'S NOTE

This book was originally published in 1974 and reflects the cultural and sexual attitudes, language, and politics of the period.

# CHAPTER ONE

It was early spring: warm and at the same time cool, greening and the dogwood had already bloomed. It was worth a drive around some of the old sections of Atlanta, and I guess some people who had done that last Sunday and would again this coming Sunday. Not me. I'm more the type to notice it if I accidentally run into a dogwood tree. I don't go out of my way.

Hump Evans is a lot like me in this. We're more the type to sit around a cool, dark bar near a front window and watch the girls on the sidewalk passing by. On this particular day we were down on the Strip, near 8th and Peachtree. It was a day when there wasn't much doing and we were between jobs, both the honest and the dishonest ones. Some weeks it's like this, and we keep a little cash squirreled away against the bad times.

Anyway, there we were in the Stein Club, and we were watching the girls prancing by and, now and then, the over-aged flower children, now dope freaks, who wandered into the Stein and out again, always as if they were looking for their best friends and couldn't quite understand why they weren't there with a large pitcher and an extra glass. It was Happy Hour. At the Stein, it's from five-thirty to six-thirty, and we'd got there early enough to take the front corner table near the juke box.

We were drinking draft beer and I was getting the bloat from it. Big as Hump is ... 6' 7" and 270 or so ... he makes a large pitcher look like his personal beer mug. In the last year or so, either his capacity has gone up or mine has gone down. That might be partly age. He's younger than I am and in better shape. Sometimes I think that, out of shape as I am, I must look like a loaf of homemade bread that's still rising and has to be kneaded a time or two more.

I'm Jim Hardman, and I used to be a cop here in Atlanta before I got some mud slung on me during a reform movement. I got the resignation in about half a step in front of the boot. I'm pudgy and over forty and deceptively mean and nasty. The dude with me is Hump Evans. For five or six years, he was right up there with the Deacon and Claude and Bubba until a knee injury finished him. He's black and a little bitter now and then, and I think we're friends, but I wouldn't say that to him. He might laugh at me, or look at me in that fuck off way of his.

The last few years, we've teamed together. We'll do almost anything that pays enough and doesn't call for eight– hour days. My girlfriend, Marcy, thinks the way I live is just lack of ambition, and if that's true, Hump has twice as much of it as I do.

Around six, this dandy came over with his glass of beer and stood in the aisle near our table, like he was looking for a place to sit. He looked about forty, with a thin pencil mustache, and he was wearing soft tweeds and had a bulldog pipe in his mouth. You could smell the sweet tobacco even over a few hippie armpits at the table next to us. After a tap dance of hesitation, he edged over to our table and nodded at the empty space next to me, against the wall.

"Mind if I sit down?"

That bothers me. I like to choose the people I drink with, but I knew the Stein was packed and I nodded, and he sat down. Now it was just a matter of letting him know that, just because he was at the table, it didn't mean we wanted a conversation with him. For a couple of minutes I thought he'd read us and got our message. It turned out he hadn't.

"It's interesting, out on the street," he said.

I nodded and looked away. I've found the best way of discouraging conversation with strangers is a vague nod or shake of the head, no matter what they say. Never a yes or a no.

"Sisyphus," the man said.

Hump turned then and looked at him. I'd heard it, too, the giveaway in his voice. Real fay. Not that I had anything against homosexuals. My brother could be one if he wanted to, just as long as he didn't talk to me while I'm drinking.

I gave the guy another look. With my way of making bad guesses, I decided he was probably an English prof at Georgia State or Tech.

"Huh?" Hump said finally.

"I like to watch them also," the guy said.

But, I thought to myself, you probably watch the boys.

"You know the myth of Sisyphus, don't you?" And then, without waiting to let Hump answer, he went on. "The king who was condemned to push a large boulder up a hill in Hades. When it would almost reach the top, it would roll back down the hill and he'd have to push it up again. Over and over. Through all eternity."

"So what?" Hump said.

"That's what they're like." He leaned past me and waved his pipe at the street people passing outside the window. "They're condemned to walk that three or four blocks of the Strip, from 6th to 10th. They push the rock from 6th to 10th, and then it rolls back down, and then they walk back to 6th and grasp the rock and push it back to 10th."

"What does all that mean?" Hump looked at him with the simple, put-on look of his.

"It's a metaphor for futility," the guy said, leaning back from in front of me.

"Is that right? Futility? That's the straight word? That's what you see outside that window?"

"Well…"

"What I see out there is girl–ass and girl–titty," Hump said, "and I don't see any futility in that, unless you're not getting any of it."

Our man read the handwriting then and found himself another table. The scent of his cologne lingered after him. Hump watched him prance away, bulldog pipe tight in his teeth, back rigid with injury and insult. "The problem with these guys is that they think everybody but them was hiding behind the door when the brains were passed out."

Which meant, I guess, that we could see the futility in that march up and down the street as well as he could. At the same time, we could see the ass and the titty and, somehow, that made it easier to take.

It was later in the evening when the call came. I was sitting on the back steps, drinking my first gin and tonic of the year. That's an occasion, and I'd almost like to mark it on the calendar. My girl, Marcy, was in the kitchen a few feet away from me, cooking some beef short ribs in wine. I knew she was tippling at the bottle she'd taken the cup of wine from for the meat. It was a large bottle, a 2/5 size, of a good French Pommard. I was about to tell her to save a bit to go with supper, when the phone rang in the bedroom.

"Yeah?" I said into the phone.

"This Jim? Jim Hardman?"

"Yeah."

"This is Hubie King."

The name didn't mean anything to me. But sometimes it was that way after an afternoon of drinking with Hump. "Who?"

"Hubie King. I was in Korea with you. Same outfit."

I got it then. Hubie and I had done some time together, and we'd been hell on the beer ration, and a time or two we'd bedded down some girls in adjoining rooms. And I remembered one Christmas we'd been snowed in at a whorehouse during a blizzard. We'd come back from Korea to Japan for some R and R with a pile of money, some of which we'd won in a blackjack game on the plane. When we'd been snowed in, we'd bought out the whorehouse for Christmas Eve and Christmas Day. And on Christmas Eve, Hubie had slogged through the snowstorm and bought perfume and candy for the four girls and the *mama-san*.

The last time I'd seen Hubie had been two or three years before. He'd come to Atlanta for a Sheriff's Association meeting. After the war, he'd gone back to Anson, Georgia, and after a few years of being a deputy, he'd gotten himself elected sheriff. The reunion that evening probably hadn't been as much fun as he'd thought it would be. The last I remember, he'd wanted to know where the whores were, and I'd told him to go to a certain bar in the back of a certain run-down hotel and order a drink, and throw back the ones he didn't like.

"Sure, Hubie, how are you?"

"Fine," he said. "Look, the last time I saw you, you said you did odd jobs. You still in the business?"

"Now and then," I said.

"I think I've got something for you. A farmer outside of town has a daughter in Atlanta. At least, he thinks she's there. Wants somebody to find her for him."

"I could probably do it." I sipped at the gin and tonic.

"You be home around noon tomorrow?"

"I'll be here."

We talked a bit more after that, but we didn't have a lot to talk about. Too much had changed in both of us since that war and that Christmas in Japan. At the end, just before he hung up, he asked, "Aren't you going to thank me for sending you the job, Hardman?"

"I'll wait and see what kind of shitty job it is," I said.

❧ ❧ ❧

I was up around ten the next morning. I showered and shaved, and put on a clean, starched white shirt and a tie. I had no way of knowing what the farmer expected, and I thought I might as well be neat. If he found me with two days' whiskers and a dirt ring on my collar, he might think my prices were too high.

Right at noon, I heard him turn up my driveway and park. I opened the door and looked out. It was a 1973 pickup truck, fire-truck red, and the man getting out of it was dressed in a dark suit with a bright tie. The knot in the tie was about as big as a fist. He was around fifty, I thought, and a little humpbacked, stooped. There was a smear of gray in his hair, and he walked wide-legged, like he had one foot in each plow furrow. Under one arm, held like a football, he carried a shoebox.

I met him at the door. "Come in, Mr. ....?"

"Barrow," he said. "John Barrow." The hand that grasped mine had skin on the palm like dried-out, turned-to-iron leather.

"A beer?" I asked, when we were in the living room.

"Coffee, if you've got it," he said.

I went into the kitchen and put on the kettle. He followed me and took a seat at the kitchen table. He seemed comfortable there, so I got myself a bottle of beer and sat down across the table from him. "I understand you're looking for your daughter."

"This is her," he said. He got a picture out of his suit coat pocket and put it on the table in front of me. It was a small picture and had rough edges. It hadn't been cut evenly. When I saw the picture, I had my guess where it came from. The girl wore a dark sweater and a string of pearls, and I remembered the picture-taking days when I'd been in high school. Boys in a dark jacket and white shirt and tie, and girls in a dark sweater and a strand of pearls. He had, I thought, cut the picture from the Anson high school yearbook.

"Her name?" I asked.

"Joy Lynn Barrow."

I stared down at the picture. Blonde hair that looked thin and without any body to it. A narrow face with quiet eyes looking out. A mouth that was trying to smile but hadn't quite made it in time for the photographer.

The kettle boiled, and I made his coffee for him. When I put it in front of him, he thanked me and untied the string from around his shoebox. Before he lifted the lid, he asked, "Have you had your lunch, Mr. Hardman?"

"I just had breakfast," I said.

He took the lid off the shoebox and put it aside. He reached into the box, after folding a sheet of wax paper aside, and took out a fried chicken leg. "I can't see paying seven prices for something to eat here in town."

"Don't blame you," I said. "Now, tell me about Joy Lynn."

"She came to Atlanta a year ago … not quite a year ago. It was after the high school graduation, in June."

"To get a job?"

He shook his head and swallowed. "It was to go to a beauty and charm school."

"What's the name of the school?"

"Foster and Summers."

"The address?"

"I don't know it," he said.

"It ought to be easy to find. Professional schools are pretty well regulated by the state."

"Hubie said you'd know what to do." He finished the chicken leg and held the bone like he wasn't quite sure what to do with it. I grinned at him and got him a plate from the china shelf.

"It should be easy," I said. "In fact, though this might sound like I'm trying to talk myself out of a job, I think you can handle it yourself. Use my phone and call the school. You can get a home address and find her yourself. I cost fifty a day, and maybe twenty-five or so in expenses."

"Hubie said you didn't come cheap." The way he said it, there wasn't any condemnation of me in it. It was just a fact. "And I do appreciate what you said, but you see, I called them long–distance yesterday, and they said they'd never even heard of her at that school."

"Maybe you got the name of it wrong."

"No, it was the right one. I know it was, because I didn't want her to go, and she saved her hog money and her egg money for three years. She knew I wasn't going to give her the money. Not on the longest day there ever was. So she saved her own money, and there wasn't a thing I could do about it. And I remember sitting down across the table from her and watching her fill out the application. She was accepted about ten days later, and I watched her write them a check. It was for the first semester's tuition."

"But are you sure …?"

"Yesterday, when they said they'd never heard of her, I went in her room and found her last bank statement, the one that came after she closed out the account, and there it was. A check for $500 to Foster and Summers."

"You bring it with you?"

He hesitated. He looked at the chicken grease on his fingers. I got him a couple of paper towels. After he wiped his fingers, he got the check out of the side pocket of his suit coat.

"You mind if I keep this for a few days?" I looked the check over, and it seemed real enough. There was a FOR DEPOSIT ONLY stamp on it, and it had been accepted by The Fulton National Bank.

"Keep it long as you need it," he said.

"The time she was here in Atlanta, did you hear from her?"

"She didn't write much, but she did call her mama a few times, and she came visiting at Thanksgiving and Christmas. It was just for a day at a time and, to tell the truth, I didn't care for the way she looked, She was dressing flashy-like, and with too much make-up."

"She tell you where she was living?"

PIMP FOR THE DEAD

"She told her mama she was staying at a dormitory at the school."

"When's the last time you saw her?"

"Back in February," he said. "She came for the afternoon, on her mama's birthday."

I watched as he reached into the shoebox and got out a pork chop. It was fried hard and dark. It looked like beef jerky. He broke off a chunk of it and chewed slowly.

"I understand all this so far," I said. "It's just that I don't see why it's bothering you this much. There's probably some good explanation…"

"Two things bother me," he said, cutting me off. "Her mama went in the hospital two days ago, and when I called that school, they said they'd never heard of her at all."

I nodded. He'd told me that. "Your wife all right?"

"They cut off part of her bosom."

"What's the second thing?"

"A story a fellow in Anson told me. I got trouble even talking about it. I wouldn't even call him a friend. He's a womanizer, and he comes to Atlanta all the time. He told me he was cruising down Peachtree, near North Avenue…I think he said North Avenue…and he saw Joy Lynn dressed up and made–up like a whore. He stopped the car to say hello to her, and she came over to the car and asked him something about did he want some company. But when she saw who he was, she ran away."

"He sure it was Joy Lynn?"

"One hundred per cent," he said.

"That changes it some," I said. "But I don't know exactly what you want me to do."

"I thought I was making it clear enough." Mr. Barrow dropped the pork chop bone on the plate. Eyes down, he dug into the shoebox and brought out a thick wedge of cake. It was chocolate, with icing on it about an inch thick. "I want you to find Joy Lynn for me."

"That shouldn't be hard."

"And I want you to get her away from those white slavers, before she's ruined completely."

I just stared at him. I think my mouth might have dropped open, too. That was the first time I'd ever heard the term used seriously in my life. But there wasn't a thin red hair of humor in how he'd said it. If she'd been my daughter, I might not have seen the humor in it either.

"You got some more coffee?" He pushed the cup toward me, and I went over to the stove and made him another cup of instant. When I brought the cup back to the table, he cleared his throat and asked, "You'll do it?"

Why not? Even if it wasn't much, it was better than nothing at all. I nodded. "But it might get rough, if it's real white slavers. I can find her by myself. That might take a day or two, and that would be covered by the fifty a day and expenses. But after I find her, and if she wants to go and they don't want her to, I might need some help. I've got this friend who'd help, but it would cost another fifty a day when I'm using him."

"If you need him, you need him." He broke the cake and ate the bottom layer first. "Hubie said you'd want an advance." He ate the middle layer then and saved the top layer, the one with all the icing on it, until last.

"A hundred and fifty to start," I said. "That ought to do for a couple of days."

"It ought to." He put the top layer of the cake on the edge of the plate, where the bones were. He wiped his hands on the paper towels and got out his roll. It was thick and held together by a wide rubber band. He put the band on his wrist and counted out seven twenties and a ten. "You want to give me a receipt?"

Afterwards, I saw him out to the front yard. I waited until he was seated in the pickup truck before I brought up my last doubt. "Of course, Joy Lynn is of age. If she's happy where she is, if she's not being held against her will, dragging her out of there might involve me in kidnapping."

"Mr. Hardman, you can take my word for it. My little girl wouldn't do that unless she was being forced."

I waved him down the driveway and went back into the house. I cleaned up the remains of his shoebox lunch, opened another beer, and carried it into the backyard. Next to the beer counter at the store, it's my favorite place in the spring and summer. There are a couple of old oak trees there for shade, and back near the property line there's a raised terrace, walled in by stone. When I feel like it, I put in a few vegetables. A couple of dozen tomato plants, a few hills of squash and a couple of rows of white corn. So far I'd done nothing about the garden, and Marcy was complaining that it was past time to get the seeds in.

I sat on the terrace wall and sipped the beer. The longer I looked at the garden plot, the more the job for Barrow looked like a bad-back saver. I went into the house and called Hump. He said it was a slow day and he needed a beer, and he'd be right over. He said he liked my beer better than his, anyway.

"What do you think about white slavery?"

We were out on the back steps. It was around one-thirty and, because Hump was dressed in his best, I'd swept off the steps.

"You mean here in Atlanta?"

"Her father thinks so." I passed Hump the picture of Joy Lynn.

"What does the rest of her look like?"

"No idea," I said.

He passed the picture back to me. "I have some trouble believing that kind of shit. Too many girls'd rather make their livings on their backs. And it's a good living, and tax-free. A girl might get talked into it, but she won't get forced."

"The way I see it, too," I said.

"You get some dip-shit jobs. You know that, don't you?"

I left him out on the steps and went in and got out the Atlanta white pages and looked up the Foster and Summers Beauty and Charm School.

On the way downtown, I explained the "muscle expense" I'd sold Mr. Barrow on. Hump was just along for the ride. After he heard me out, Hump said, "That's fifty dollars I won't get to spend."

"There you go again," I said. "No faith in anything."

"That girl wants to sell her ass, that's her business. I don't see any percentage in fussing around with some hard-assed pimps about it."

"Let's assume, just for the time, that her father might be right."

"Shit," Hump said.

"Let's assume this is a new outbreak of white slavery."

"Double shit," Hump said.

I grinned at him, and he grinned back.

"For a minute there," he said, "I was starting to believe that senility had hit you a better-than-average lick."

The Foster and Summer Beauty and Charm School is on the second floor of a building on Whitehall. It is the part of Whitehall where most of the stores make their living ripping off blacks. The men's stores with the cheap and flashy duds in the window, the dress shops, the discount shoe shops. Most of it junk that must have been made especially for the rip-off business. It was time payments, and all the credit you wanted, and god knows how much interest you paid on the balance in a year.

The school was directly above a shop that specialized in cut-rate cameras and watches, Saturday Night Specials and portable radios. The special this week was a thousand bobby pins for 49 cents. I pulled to the curb across the street and got out. Hump slid over behind the wheel and said he'd park and meet me in a few minutes.

Right away, as soon as I entered the stair well, I was surprised. It was enough to make a man snow–blind. The walls and ceiling were painted a flat white, and white carpet covered the stairs. Blinking, I reached the top of the stairs and I was in the lobby. The walls there were the same white, but the effect was eased somewhat by the huge photographic blowups of high–fashion models in exaggerated, spastic poses. I did a quick count. There were eight blowups and four of the models were black. That told me something about where they got their nickels and dimes and dollars.

Straight ahead, there was a teakwood desk about as big as a bed. The girl behind it looked like she'd just stepped out of one of the blowups. The thin, tubercular body, the face with the bones about to break through the skin, her hair in those godawful Shirley Temple curls.

She looked me up and down and read the price tag on my suit. That didn't mean much to her, either way. Not rich, not poor. "Can I help you?"

"I'm John Barrow. I'm from Anson, and I called the other day to get in touch with my daughter, Joy Lynn, and you said you'd never heard of her."

"Is she in our school?"

"She's supposed to be," I said.

"I don't remember the call. When was that?"

"Yesterday," I said.

"I don't remember …"

"I don't give a shit what you remember," I said. "My daughter's supposed to be in this school, and somebody here said they'd never even heard of her."

"I'll check." She got up from behind the desk, and I watched her walk to the circular index file on a shelf against the wall.

Bones that would cut you in bed like a dull knife-edge. Not my type, at all. "Did you say Barrow?"

"Joy Lynn Barrow."

She checked and double checked. "We have no one by that name enrolled in our school."

"Not now, or not ever?"

"The file is for past and present students, and there is no Joy Lynn Barrow there."

"She started last summer," I said.

"Not with us."

I reached in my pocket and got out the canceled check. I leaned across the desk and showed her the front and back of it. "Explain this to me, then."

She gave me a puzzled look. "That's odd."

"A bit," I said.

"I think you'd better speak to our bursar, Mr. Franklin."

"Might as well."

She led me down a hallway. All the doors were closed, except for the one directly at the end of it. Just outside the door, she waved me to a stop and went in and closed the door behind her. I edged up to the door, but it was a short conversation and she must have been whispering. I watched the doorknob and, when it turned, I backed away.

"Mr. Franklin will see you now."

It was a big office. The walls had started out white, like the rest of the place, but somebody had done a sort of Peter Max all over the walls in ropes of red and black and yellow. The man behind the desk was slim, very slight, and deeply tanned. He was wearing a red blazer with huge silver buttons, a silver gray shirt, and a polka dot red-and-white ascot. He looked dwarfed by the desk, and I made my guess that he probably wore elevator shoes.

"Yes, Mr. ...?"

"Barrow," I said. "John Barrow."

He offered his hand and I got a clammy touch of it. It was like a girl's was supposed to be, creamy and tender as a baby's. "Miss Hunter said you have some mistaken belief that your daughter is or was enrolled at our school."

"If it's a mistake, it's not mine."

"She said our records…"

"I've got the check to prove it," I said. I got out the check again and gave him a slow look at both sides. Franklin didn't seem as bothered by it as the girl out at the desk had been.

"You saw Miss Hunter look in our files?"

I nodded.

"Then it's probably quite simple." He pushed back his chair and stood up. I gave myself the prize. He was wearing elevator shoes. "If she is not in the front file, it is quite possible she never matriculated." He reached a file cabinet and unlocked and drew out the top drawer.

"What does that mean?"

"It means she dropped out without ever really attending a class," he said. "You said Barrow, didn't you?"

"Yes."

His face away from me, he worked through a thin stack of folders. His fingers stopped. "Joy Lynn?" he asked.

"That's her."

He pulled the file out and held it so that I couldn't see the tab on it. He opened it and read for a few seconds before he nodded to himself and lifted his eyes. "I remember now. Your daughter did make application and she was accepted. On June 12th, two days before her classes were to begin, she came by to see me. I don't remember her, but my notes say that I talked to her. She'd changed her mind and she wanted her tuition back. She was given a check for four hundred and fifty dollars. The other fifty dollars we held back to cover our expenses." He closed the folder. "That would explain why she isn't in the file in the lobby. She never really entered the school."

"You mail the check to her?"

"What?"

"You have an address?"

"We gave her a check that same day," he said.

"Is that usual?"

"No, but she insisted."

I took a step toward him. "You mind if I see that folder?"

"These files are not open to public inspection." He leaned over quickly, jammed the file into the drawer, and slammed it shut. He slammed in the lock with the palm of a tiny hand.

"I'd like some real proof that my daughter received her refund."

"Your daughter will verify that," he said.

"Your canceled check would, too," I said.

"That is a matter for our bookkeeper...and she is on vacation." He returned to his chair and sat down. "Is that all, Mr. Barrow?"

"For the time," I said. "Unless I find you've been lying to me."

"Good day, then."

I went back down the hallway and into the lobby. The girl behind the desk looked at me like she couldn't remember exactly where she'd seen me before. Or if she had ever seen me before.

"And you didn't believe him?"

"Maybe," I said, "and maybe not."

"It sounds possible. Girl comes to town, this pimp meets her and starts chewing on her and sucking her blood. He tells her she don't need any beauty and charm school, so why don't she get her pretty ass on down there and get that tuition money back?"

We'd left the car in the parking lot and walked down a block or two, and down the steps into Underground Atlanta. At the Crêpes de Paris, we'd had a martini and, after that, a fresh mushroom salad and the crepes with shrimp and a creamy sauce, and a bottle of a dry white wine.

"I'd like to kick his ass. I didn't like his fucking attitude." I sipped at my coffee. "Maybe it was because he was a midget. You know how little men act."

Hump smiled and broke it off in me. "To me, you're a little man, too."

"You got plans for the evening?"

"Nothing much," he said.

"I thought we'd do some whore-hunting. That cocksman friend of Barrow's said he saw Joy Lynn at North Avenue and Peachtree. It might be worth a try, cruising by there a few times tonight."

"It's Friday," Hump said, "and they'll be out after the week-end dollar."

I drove home and dropped him next to his car. I said I'd pick him up at eight. After he drove away, I walked around the house and up to the terrace, where the garden plot was. It was pretty badly grown over, and there were dead limbs from the winter. Grass and stinking weeds. Just looking at it made me tired. I decided I'd take another day to think about it and, if I got any more static from Marcy, I'd hire somebody to clear it and break up the ground and turn it.

That decision made and off my back, I went into the house and took a three-hour nap.

It was a couple of minutes after eight when I pulled up in front of Hump's apartment house. He was standing out by the steps, smoking a cigarette and watching the traffic go by. He tossed his smoke in the gutter and headed around the front of my car for the passenger seat.

"You drive," I said.

He got behind the wheel. "For any good reason?"

"In case we see Joy Lynn. I want to be able to step out in a hurry and have my few words with her."

For the next hour or so, we made a circuit from Linden Avenue, where Crawford Long Hospital is, down to Peachtree Place. Peachtree Place is the old 9th Street, so we were covering a good part of the Strip. There was a lot of whore action but no sign of Joy Lynn. Unless we'd missed her. That was possible, if she'd done something with her hair or was wearing a wig. I just hoped she hadn't. Barrow's friend had recognized her right away, and I guess that meant there hadn't been any disguise that he'd had to work his way through.

It must have been the fifth or sixth time around ... with time out for a couple of beers ... when I thought I'd spotted her. It was in front of the Aetna Loan Company. That's at the corner of Ponce de Leon and Peach-tree, across from the Hotel Georgian Terrace.

"There," I said.

It did look like her. The same wispy hair, the long, thin face. She was wearing white hot-pants and a red blouse and clogs. She carried a huge shoulder bag that was about the size of a beach bag. God knows what she needed to carry in it. Maybe everything from a change of underwear to an inflatable mattress.

"Not alone," Hump said.

It was a brief look, and I'd been spending most of it on the girl I thought might be Joy Lynn Barrow. I had, I guess, seen the girl with her. And I was shaking my head, trying to throw all the ghost images out. The girl with her was a dwarf. Either that, or she'd been standing on her kneecaps.

We were headed toward the Linden Avenue turn on our circuit. "You see it the way I did?" I asked Hump.

"Both of us can't be crazy at the same time," he said.

He did his turn onto Linden, and then jogged right onto West Peachtree. We followed that until we reached 3rd Street. At 3rd, he took another right to Peachtree and hooked right one more time, and we were heading for the corner where we'd seen them. He stayed in the curb lane and slowed when we passed the Fox Theater. At the corner, right in the bus-stop lane, he touched the horn and stopped near the two girls. The girls were backed against the Aetna Loan Company window. They didn't move. Hump touched the horn again, and I rolled down the window on the curb side. The girl I thought was Joy Lynn said something to the dwarf girl and pushed away from the window. She reached the car and leaned over to look at me.

"You girls want to take a ride with us?"

"I don't want you to misunderstand us," the girl said. That was her way of telling me it was play for pay, without saying anything that could be used in court if we turned out to be vice squad.

"I understand," I said.

Up close, I was pretty certain it was Joy Lynn. She looked right, and the accent was right, too. I looked over at Hump, and both of us watched her walk over to the dwarf girl. Good body, and she was showing almost more than was legal. Long, slim legs with a slight bow, and a tight, hard ass.

"Nice," Hump said. "She's got something to sell."

Behind us, some of the cars in our lane started honking at us, wanting us to move on, now that the light had changed again. Hump put out an arm and waved them around us. They were still honking when they passed.

The girls got into the back seat. Hump pulled away and headed up Peachtree. I put an arm on the back of the seat and turned to face the girls. "I'm Jim and this is Hump."

"I'm Linda," the blonde girl said. Next to her, the dwarf girl perched on the edge of the seat, her feet not touching the floor. In the light of the street lamps, I could see that she seemed in good proportion, and her face was regular and attractive in a childlike way. "And this is Carol."

"Hi," the dwarf girl said.

The light ahead went red, and Hump stopped. He turned and looked at Carol. "Lord, you're a short drink of water."

"But worth it all," she said.

"You say," Hump said.

"Try me," Carol said.

The blonde, Linda or Joy Lynn, or whatever, leaned forward, and I could see her wetting her lips. "It's forty," she said.

"I don't want to waste much of your time," I said. It was time to get on with it. "You're Joy Lynn Barrow, aren't you?"

She leaned away. "What do you want?"

The light changed, and Hump pulled away. I turned to him and said, under my breath, "Keep it moving." I was just in time. She grabbed the door handle and then found we were moving too fast. She released the handle and leaned back in the seat.

"What do you want?"

"Your father wants to know what you're up to. He tried to reach you at the school and couldn't."

"Why?"

"Why what?"

"Why did he want to reach me?"

"Your mother's had an operation. It might be serious. From what he said, it sounded like breast cancer."

"All right," she said.

"All right what?"

"You've told me. Now you can drop us back on our corner."

"He's got a funny idea that the white slavers got you," I said.

"He would. God, how stupid and country can you be?"

I grinned at her. "And the white slavers don't have you?"

"I'm fine. Nobody forced me. I like it. I like sleeping all day and screwing all night. You tell him that."

I nodded at Hump. "Take us back."

"Who are you?" Joy Lynn asked.

"A friend of the sheriff back in Anson."

"A cop?"

"Not any more," I said.

The dwarf girl, Carol, said, "This is some shit, wasting our time like this."

"It don't have to be a waste," Hump said, "if you're giving free samples."

"Baby, there ain't no such thing."

"You freelancing, or you got a pimp?" I asked of Joy Lynn.

"It's not much of your business, either way."

"I'd guess a pimp."

"And a damn good one, too," Joy Lynn said. "If he knew you'd been bothering me, he'd kick your fat ass."

"Maybe. Maybe not. I never thought much of the balls on a guy who lives off women."

"I'd like to be there and hear you tell him that," she said.

"A lot of interesting things never happen."

Hump worked his way back into the same circuit, though an elongated one now, and a few minutes later we were back in the same bus-stop lane. As soon as the car stopped, Joy Lynn had the door open and was out on the pavement. Carol followed her. Joy Lynn waited until she was clear and slammed the door.

Hump was ready to pull away when I touched his shoulder. "Wait one." I got out and walked over to Joy Lynn.

"What now?" The hard go-to-hell was in her voice.

"What you do is your business, and I'll talk to your father and try to make him see it. Maybe I can get him to give it up. But I've got a price."

"What price?"

"Give your mother a call at the hospital, and tell her you're all right."

"That's all?"

"That's all," I said.

"I'll call her in the morning."

"And I'll talk to your father." I turned and walked away.

"I'm not going to thank you," she yelled after me.

"I didn't expect it."

I should have seen it then. I was heading back to the car, and I looked up at the light and it changed. Hump had the red now, and the green was for cars coming out of Ponce de Leon, toward me. A black Fury was in front, and it gunned its engine and took a leap over the crosswalk lines. It headed toward the corner where I was, in the lane that would bring it near the curb. The window in back was down and, as it got close to me, I saw something sticking out and braced against the window ledge. At first I didn't read that it was the barrel of a pump shotgun. Then it was too late. My first thought was that it was for me, and then I didn't have time to worry about it.

I yelled over my shoulder, "Get down!" and then I hit the pavement on my knees and belly, and rolled toward my car.

Behind me I heard the *crump, crump, crump,* and I thought I heard one of the girls scream, but I couldn't be sure. I heard breaking glass and, across the street, in front of the Hotel Georgian Terrace, a woman started screaming a long, high scream that didn't have any pauses in it for breath.

I heard the Fury gun its engine again and rubber squealed, and I turned over and looked in the direction of the girls. Both of them were down. I got up and ran for them. Down the street, the tail lights of the Fury winked once at me, and then it took a right and was gone out West Peachtree.

Joy Lynn was a mess. She'd caught a full blast in the upper chest, neck and face. Her chin was gone, just mush. I tried for a pulse and couldn't find one. I duck-walked away from her, over to the dwarf girl, Carol. She'd caught it in the chest and shoulder, and I could hear a low moan out of her. Looking up, I saw Hump standing over me.

"Call the police and tell them to send an ambulance," I said. "I think this one is still alive."

Carol lived only a couple of minutes more. She wasn't alive when the ambulance arrived. Messed up as she was, I was amazed that she lasted as long as she did. I guess it was being a dwarf, being used to adversity, that kept her alive the extra time.

# CHAPTER TWO

Art Maloney, his flat Irish face thoughtful, watched the detachment from the fire department hose down the sidewalk and try to blast the pooled blood and tissue from the pavement and lower wall. The water didn't get it all. A brush might have helped, but they didn't bother. I knew if I passed the corner the next day, there'd be the ghost of the stain still there.

"So you were out cruising whores?" he said to me.

"I told you," I said.

"What does Marcy think of all this?"

It was his way of needling me. Art thought a hell of a lot of Marcy, and he was a Catholic, and he kept nibbling around the edges, trying to find out when we were going to get married. Since there never was an answer he liked, he always tried to make me out the biggest asshole in the world. Aside from that he was a good friend, and our friendship went back to our time on the force. I'd left, but he'd stayed on.

"Marcy approves," I said. "She read somewhere that a man is not naturally monogamous."

"You got money to spring for a drink?"

I looked over at Hump, who was standing next to my car, still in the bus-stop lane. "I don't want to be towed."

A uniformed cop stood next to the shattered window of the loan office. He was waiting for the team of carpenters to arrive and board over the window until morning.

Art said, "Keep an eye on that car." And then, to me, "How about across the street?"

We crossed the street to the Hotel Georgian Terrace. The hotel had been an Atlanta landmark in its time. Enrico Caruso had said it was his favorite hotel in the whole world when he'd come to town with the Met, but that was a long time ago. Now it was held together by new wallpaper and paste.

The lounge at the front corner had changed names a number of times. It had been the Purple Poodle for a year or so, and now it was the Venetian Lounge. It was about the same inside. It was easier to change the name than spend huge amounts on renovations. Art motioned toward a table away from the jukebox.

The drinks came a few minutes later, and the waitress looked at, the change from a five like it was black plague germs I was offering her. Art waited until she did her angry march away from the table. "You going to call the father?"

I shook my head. "I'll call Hubie. He can break the news in person. I don't think he's going to like it."

Art sipped his Irish over the rocks and opened a note pad. "Who was the dwarf girl?"

"All I got was the first name. Carol."

"You check the purses?" Hump asked.

"Not much in there. Almost nothing with a name on it. No home address, either." He nodded at me. "There was one thing. A letter without the envelope, addressed to Carol, from somebody named Edwin Spinks, and with an A.P.O. number. We'll check it out."

"That usual with prosties?"

"Not carrying much identification? It seems to be a trend. They get ripped off. Why carry around anything they might have to replace later?"

"I'd like to talk to her pimp," I said.

"That's a fat chance. You think some pimp's going to walk in and say that was part of his stable got torn up out there?"

"It might be hard to tab him. Might not, though. Take the dwarf girl. She might be the key. You ask about a blonde and who her pimp was. What blonde? What pimp? But you throw in the dwarf girl who was always with the blonde, and somebody might know who the pimp was."

"If the dwarf was always with her," Art said.

"Have to play it that way, and hope."

"Too bad you're out of a job now. It's your kind of work."

"Easy enough for you to check out, Art."

Art shook his head. "Tonight's Friday. You know how many killings we'll have by Monday? Maybe five or six. I can't spend that time on just one of them."

"Not on a prostie," I said. "Now if it was a banker from downtown."

"It would be different," Art said.

"You bet your ass it would be." I sipped my drink. "Now that I'm out of a job, I wonder why I'm buying you a drink?"

"A bribe," Art said. "That's so I don't take you downtown and turn you over to a wrecking crew."

I grinned at him. "I'm glad I wasn't around in those days. A lot of people who got arrested used to try to escape. And used to get subdued."

"Lots of bruises and lots of confessions," Art said.

"Or just some lumps that told some guy not to fuck around in this cop's territory anymore."

"It sounds like primitive police work," Hump said.

"Basic."

"How'd it work?" Hump asked.

Art leaned back in his chair. "Take this pimp. We pick him up, and he says he never heard of these two girls. So I put him in with a wrecking crew, and they beat the pure living crap out of him. First thing you know, he does remember those girls, including how much money they made last year for him, and how many tricks they turned."

"But now he's got bruises," Hump said.

"Missing teeth, and broken bones, and all that. But we've got four cops who say he tried to escape. And they make a report about how violent he got."

"And how they used just enough force to subdue him," I said.

"It was different then," Art said. "Being a criminal meant you didn't have any rights."

"I'd still like to talk to that pimp."

"Do it on your own time," Art said.

I lifted my right leg and showed him the tear at the knee of the pants and the bloodstains on the cuff. "It's already cost me a thirty-dollar pair of pants."

Art pushed his empty glass at me. "Was that invitation for a drink or drinks?"

I ordered another round.

I called Hubie and reached him at home. I laid it out for him and listened to him grumble and bitch for a few minutes. It was a twenty-mile drive out to the Barrow place, and he didn't like leaving his backyard, or his bottle, or whatever.

I took the bitch and the grumble. They were his wages for a shitty job.

It was almost midnight when he called me back. "Right back to you, Jim."

"How?"

"John Barrow's heading your way tomorrow. He had a call while I was there. Atlanta police want an ID from him."

At least that was good timing. They hadn't called before Hubie got there to break the bad news. "What's that got to do with me?"

"He's going to stop by your place afterwards."

Oh, shit.

"Thought you'd like that," Hubie said.

It wasn't like the usual Saturday. I was up early. Frustrated and mean as a snake. I had my coffee out on the back steps, feeling that early spring coolness. It took me about an hour to get it up, and then I changed to some work clothes. It took me another half-hour to get past the looking-and-trying-to-decide-what-to-do stage.

But once I started, it went well. I got all the dead limbs out of the terrace plot first, and stacked them. After that, I used a spade and started to break ground. It was slow and hard work, and even gloves didn't do much to protect my hands. I could feel the blisters coming up. I didn't have to take the gloves off to know I had fat ones on the palms of my hands and narrow, banded ones on the yokes between my thumbs and first fingers.

I was halfway through the plot by noon, and I took time off to make a couple of sandwiches and a big pitcher of iced tea, I'd finished the sandwiches and most of the tea when Mr. Barrow found me. He must have tried the front door first and then, seeing my car still there, walked around to the backyard.

I waved at him and sat on the stone wall at the front of the terrace and watched him come up the slope toward me. It looked like the energy had gone out of him. He was stooped more now, and his feet dragged. We gave each other brief nods, not speaking, and he looked at the work I'd done so far while I went down to the kitchen and got a tea glass for him. I poured a glass of tea for him and put it on the wall near him. He had a clump of the dirt I'd dug up in his hands, feeling it and smelling it.

"What you going to plant?"

I told him, and he rubbed the dirt between his hands and poured it out in single grains.

"Needs some manure," he said.

"I'll put some on," I said. "Sheep all right?"

He nodded. He noticed the tea, lifted the glass, and gave it a courtesy sip. "Hubie said you talked to her before it happened."

"I know it won't mean much now," I said, "but she was going to call her mother this morning. She said she was going to."

"Wish she could have. Emily's taking it hard."

"I took it hard myself," I said. "She was a pretty, young girl, and I never get used to that ... that violence happening."

"God damn," he said suddenly. "God fucking damn."

I looked at him and then looked away. I hadn't known why he wanted to see me. I didn't think it was to get back part of the advance he'd given me. Maybe it was. You just couldn't tell. But part of it was that he wanted to let the frustration and anger out. He had a sick wife at home, and he couldn't do it there. But here I was, hired by him, and it might be his way of getting his money's worth.

But I was wrong. He covered it over as soon as it broke out. He looked at my garden plot. "You got another spade?"

I shook my head.

"A rake?"

"Yeah," I said.

"I'll dig. You break it up and rake it out."

I came back from the garage with the rake and found him, without his jacket and with his sleeves rolled up, digging away where I'd left off. I went back over to where I'd started and used the rake to break up the clumps and work the grass and weeds out. He worked steadily for an hour, not saying anything, just demon-driven and intent. At the end of the hour he dropped the spade and went over and sat on the terrace ledge. I went down and refilled the pitcher with tea and ice cubes and came back up the slope. He was breathing hard, like a cat or a dog does in hot weather, but he was hardly sweating. He drank one glass of tea at a gulp and held out his glass for another.

"You know," he said, "she wasn't really our daughter. She was adopted."

"That doesn't change anything."

"I remember her as a baby. Hardly as big as a minute."

I nodded.

"I wanted a son, but for some reason we couldn't have one. And when we decided to adopt a baby I still wanted a son, but Emily took one look at that baby, and she wanted that one so much I couldn't deny it to her."

"You could have adopted a boy, too," I said.

He looked at me for a long moment, as if he wasn't sure which one of us was the crazy one. "It bothered me, the child's breeding. Not knowing who the baby's parents were, and what you could expect when the baby grew up."

"Children aren't like pigs and cows," I said.

"Yes, they are. Oh, I got told different at the time. Doctor Rogers... he was our doctor in Anson, until he died two years ago... I asked him, and he said heredity didn't count in people any more. He said it was environment that was important, how a child was loved, and how it grew up. And I tried to believe him."

"But you don't any more?"

"Not any more."

"I don't see how it matters," I said.

"It matters. You don't know how I loved that little girl. I even got over her not being the son I wanted. You had to see her at five and six and seven to know. And right on up until she was in the ninth grade. But then something happened, and she wasn't the same any more."

I made my guess. "She found out you weren't her real parents?"

He nodded. "It liked to tore the heart out of her."

"How'd she find out?"

"I don't know. One morning she left for school and everything was fine. When she came home that afternoon it was all different."

"How?"

"She asked her mama who her real mama and daddy were."

"Just straight out?" I asked.

He nodded. "For a time I thought she'd got over it. I guess that was just what showed on the outside. It was then she started saving her money to move to Atlanta."

"Still affectionate? Still seemed to care for you and your wife?"

"It looked that way, but I guess it was put on."

I decided I'd better go ahead and get it over with. "What still bothers you?"

"I knew better than to adopt her. I just knew it. I knew there'd come a time we'd end up paying for somebody else's mistakes in bed."

"That's a harsh way of talking about her now," I said.

"I know it."

His eyes got that faraway look and I couldn't see the pictures in his mind. I thought I knew what they were. The child at six and seven and eight. The innocent love a child gives to a couple who need it. The whole fifteen years before it changes and goes down the drain. I watched the calmness in his face, and I don't think he was seeing it after Joy Lynn knew the truth.

"You know how much land I've got?"

"No," I said.

"About eight hundred acres. You know what they're worth?"

I shook my head.

"A quarter of a million dollars. That's just the land."

"That's a lot of land." I knew that sounded lame, but I didn't know where the conversation was taking us.

"I've got almost no need for it now."

"There's your wife," I said.

"The doctors give her a year, at most. Might be less than a year. The cancer's spreading."

"Sorry." I looked away.

"I went by the bank this morning." He reached into his pocket. The roll of money was about the same thickness, but this time there were hundred-dollar bills on top. "I asked about you. I asked Hubie about you, and then I had him make some calls to the Atlanta police. What I heard was mixed. Some don't like you, and some don't know for sure if you're honest. But most of them say you're a damned good man when it comes to figuring out things."

He took the rubber band from the roll. His hand was shaking so much, the rubber band got away from him and flew up into the garden plot. He started counting out hundred-dollar bills. He reached a thousand and went right past it. He stopped at two thousand.

"Is that enough?"

"For me and my partner, both," I said.

"There's more, if you need it." He stood up and shoved the rest of the roll deep into his pocket. "I want to hear from you soon."

"You'll hear from me."

"I want to know what happened to her, and why. I want to look him in the face."

The hundred-dollar bills were on the stone ledge between us. A breeze ruffled them, but they remained in place.

He folded the jacket over his arm and walked down the slope without looking back. I sat there and saw him round the side of the house and go out of sight. A minute later, I heard the pickup fire up in the driveway.

I fanned the hundreds. A breeze blew down the yard, chilling the sweat on my body. I closed the fan of hundreds and stuffed them in a damp pocket. I got the spade and the rake and stored them back in the garage. In the house, I showered and stretched out on the bed for an hour or so. The hour turned into three and, about supper time, back stiff and hands sore, I rolled to the edge of the bed and called Hump.

"We've got money and we've got work," I said.

"There's this trim who wants some of me tonight," Hump said.

"I want to start now, not tomorrow morning."

"Now you're talking like a boss white."

"I didn't mean to," I said.

"No damage," he said evenly. "That girl can hold it for me until midnight."

"You sure?"

"Sure enough."

He hung up and I got dressed.

# CHAPTER THREE

"I know three places," Hump said, "but you're not going to be welcome in any of them." He took a last smiling look at the ten hundred-dollar bills and folded them and put them in his right front pants pocket.

"Black?"

"Joy Lynn didn't give us the color of her pimp, did she?"

"Not exactly."

"Got to check some addresses." Hump left and went into the bedroom. He brought back the white pages of the phone book. "You see, there are some key words. They're like a code. The words are *sporting, sport* and *player.* All of them are tied up in the pimp's world. You find a bar or a club with one of them attached to the name somehow or other, and there's a better than average chance you're going to find about twenty or thirty pimps standing around drinking and flashing their clothes and bragging about their stable of expensive and faithful foxes."

I dropped his empty beer bottle in the trash and opened him another. I put it next to his elbow and leaned over his shoulder while he wrote down three places: *Sport's Lounge, Sporting Life* and *Player's Place.* That done, he flipped through the directory pages and wrote down the addresses. The first one was on Piedmont, the second on Reardon, and the last one on Pryor. I knew the town pretty well, but I couldn't remember ever having passed even one of the three.

Hump pushed the phone book away and stood up. "I'll take the beer with me. What are you going to do?"

"I thought I'd go with you."

He shook his head. "I'm going to have enough trouble working my way around to asking questions. With you along, looking like a cop, I might have to fight my way out of a couple of these places."

"I can stay here and drink."

"Blacks aren't the only pimps in town," Hump said. "Check out some of the white ones."

"You got any names?"

"Try Willie Whitman."

"He pimping?" The whole idea of that confused me. The last I'd heard of Willie, he'd been doing cons on farmers. In fact, you hardly heard of him at all until the summer months. That was when the cotton and the tobacco got sold, and the farmers had some cash money. Willie had the pigeon drop, and a hundred versions of that, and selling farmers' wives big, beautiful appliances that never arrived.

"Not pimping," Hump said. "Selling information. Last year, he tried a new kind of pigeon drop on a hard-assed young farmer, and the farmer busted him up some."

"Where'll I find him?"

"Try the Hollywood Bar on Peachtree near 10th. He's drinking with the winos now."

I followed him to the front door. "When'll you be back?"

"Might be midnight. Can't rush this kind of thing."

Without realizing I was doing it, I was rubbing the blisters on the palms of my hands. Hump saw what I was doing and grinned at me. "You a farmer. That's a laugh."

"Laugh at my tomatoes, my squash and my corn."

"If I ever see them," Hump said.

I called Marcy after Hump left. I think I caught her in the bath. "You want to play detective with me?"

"You serious, Jim?" She laughed. "Is it like playing doctor?"

"One hundred per cent."

I told her to dress like she was going on a picnic. I didn't want the clothing to be expensive. Jeans, a blouse and a sweater. "Be kind of coarse-looking," I said at the end.

"Bastard."

I didn't recognize Willie at first. I ordered a pitcher of beer at the bar and, while I waited for the bartender to draw it, I had my casual look around. Three winos at the end of the bar near the front door. He wasn't in that group. Two near me. Not in there. And there was one at the back end of the bar, facing away from me.

The Hollywood is just a few doors down from the House of Eng, a good Chinese restaurant, but about a thousand real miles separate them. The Hollywood is for the lost ones, the ones who are barred from most of the other taverns in town. They sit over their bottle or pitcher like a man over his last meal. Make it last, taste every drop.

I lifted the pitcher and was heading for the booth where Marcy was, when the man at the back end of the bar turned on his stool and looked at me. It was Willie Whitman. But a battered and changed one. His nose was pushed out of line and needed an operation. The ear next to me looked like a butternut squash. The farmer had really ruined him. I couldn't see anybody buying a used car from him. And I couldn't see him doing the pigeon drop without plastic surgery.

He looked away without even a nod, and I went along with him. I put my back to him, went over to the booth, and poured Marcy a glass of beer.

"I like your idea of a night on the town," Marcy said.

"It's got the best country and western jukebox in town."

"You promised me supper," she said, shrill and a bit off-key. That was Marcy's idea of acting, but a couple of winos turned in their seats and looked at us.

"Oh, shut up, Ethel," I said. Shaking the change in my pockets, I walked back to the jukebox and dropped a couple of quarters in. I played some Merle Haggard and Tom T. Hall. When I turned away from the jukebox, Merle was singing about being a branded man. I looked at Willie Whitman. "Women," I said, loud enough to be heard all the way down the bar.

"Can't live with 'em, can't live without 'em," Willie said.

"Damn right." I put an elbow on the bar next to him. I saw Willie was drinking a Bud. I waved at the bartender and he came down. "Give my friend here a beer." The bartender, just like he would have at a better place, looked at Willie and Willie nodded. I got out my roll and paid for it with a single. But I worked it until a twenty was on top. Willie saw the twenty.

"Hardman, how are you?" he said under his breath.

"Working," I said.

"I'm not. I'm down on it, right now."

"I heard."

The bartender brought the Bud and I waved the change away. Willie waited until the bartender moved away. "What are you working on?"

"The two hookers who got shot last night on Peachtree and Ponce de Leon."

"That's a bad one," Willie said.

Marcy decided to try out her acting again. "Jim," she yelled, "you going to leave me by myself all night?"

"Shut up, Ethel," I said back to her. "I'll be there when I get there." And just to show I wasn't about to be bossed around by a woman, I lifted Willie's beer bottle and pointed to myself. The bartender brought me a Bud and a glass. After he took my money, he leaned toward me.

"She's not going to make trouble, is she?"

"Not a chance," I said, "but I'll make sure." I swaggered down the aisle to the booth. Marcy looked up at me. "I'm talking to a friend back there. If you're hungry, go over to Eng's and order yourself a chow mein sandwich. I'll be there as soon as I'm ready."

"I'll wait," she said.

"Then hold it down. You're bothering the bartender." I walked back down to Willie. I lifted the bottle and drank from it. The bartender winked at me and moved away. As far as he was concerned, I was just showing a cunt where she stood. He could understand that. And now he would think that any conversation with the old wino was my way of twisting the knife a little.

"You know anything about the two girls last night?"

"Just what I read in the paper," Willie said.

"I've got a twenty."

"I could use the twenty. I just don't know anything worth it."

"I'll settle for the names of a couple of white pimps whose girls work this area."

"That's easier."

I reached in my pocket and worked the twenty free. I folded it a couple of times and brought it out. Willie looked down at it and nodded.

"Know one. Big white dude. A mean-ass. Name's Wash Johnson."

"Where can I find him?"

"Most nights, he's at 590 West," Willie said.

"The top of the new Stouffer's? That high up?"

"He doesn't work it. It's where he hangs out. Mainly at the bar. It's his stop, so his girls can reach him if they need to."

"How'll I know him?"

"Like I said, big dude, blond hair, shoulders like a linebacker."

"How old?"

"About 25 or 26."

"Thanks, Willie." I dropped the hand and tapped the twenty against his knee. His hand closed over it like a claw. I patted his shoulder and walked back to my booth. I sat across the table from Marcy and winked. Even dressed for the acting job, she looked damned good for a woman past thirty.

"Act one's over, and you're not in act two," I said. "How about some Chinese?"

"Ethel?" she said when we were out on the street. "Did it have to be Ethel?"

"You looked like an Ethel," I said.

After supper at Eng's she didn't want to go back to her apartment. I gave her my house key and put her in a cab. I kept a tie in the glove compartment of my car. I put that on, and hoped I'd get past the hostess at the elevator. Without the tie, I looked a little seedy. With it, I didn't look much better.

I picked Wash Johnson out from a distance. He matched the description Willie had given me. He did have the shoulders, and a blocky, squarish face. Tonight he was wearing a red hopsack jacket and gray flared trousers. There was a Bloody Mary in front of him. Seats on both sides of him were empty. I walked over and took the seat on his right.

I ordered a Bloody Mary, too. It came dressed with a celery stirrer, and I chewed at the celery and tried to think of some way of starting a conversation with Wash. He hadn't taken any notice of me when I first sat down or when I'd ordered. Wash was at the end of the bar that was nearest the huge windows. He was watching the cars on the street, some twenty-five or twenty-six floors down.

It turned out that I didn't have to do anything elaborate, like spilling my drink on him. He swung his shoulders around and stared at me. "I know you from somewhere." The way he said it didn't sound like what he might know would make us friends.

"Jim Hardman," I said.

"Used to be a cop."

"Until a few years ago," I said.

"You here for any reason?"

"I'm drinking a Bloody Mary."

I spent the silence that brought on by looking over 590 West. I'd brought Marcy up here right after it opened. It was a little too plastic and new for our tastes. I guess I like the old bars better. It was a wide room with a good many tables near the window, so you could look down on absolutely nothing. Until the skyline changed in Atlanta, it probably wasn't worth the tab.

"You were on the street last night when the two girls got it," Wash said.

"My bad luck," I said.

"You don't look as bad as they do."

"Skinned a knee," I said.

"I think you came up here to ask me something. Right?"

"I wondered if the girls were out of your stable."

That got his shoulders tight. "What makes you think I've got a stable?"

"It's the word on the street."

"The word on the street's full of shit," Wash said.

"If you say so," I said, giving it my best bored pitch. "It's nothing to me. A friend from the old days on the force is handling the case. He can ask you the questions. I'll pass your name on to him, and he'll be at your house tonight before the sheets get warm."

"That sounds like a threat to me."

"Me threaten you? Shit, what's the percentage in that?"

"I wouldn't like to be pulled in," Wash said. "That could piss me off a bit."

I could see the muscle working under the coat. If he kept up the demonstration, he was going to pop a seam or two.

"It's like this. The Barrow girl's old country daddy wants to know what his daughter was doing out there, whoring on the street. I'd like to talk to the guy who turned her out ... that's all."

"It wasn't me."

I nodded. "But you didn't say you don't know who he is."

"I don't know," Wash said.

"You know."

He took the celery stirrer from his Bloody Mary and chewed on it angrily. When he reached the nub, he dropped it in the ash tray in front of him. "You mess around on the street out there, you could end up trying to grin at that shotgun."

"Now it sounds like you're threatening me."

"Not from me." He lowered his voice. "It's getting bad out there. Somebody wants to start a pimp's union and charge dues."

"You been approached?"

"No comment, like they say on the TV."

"So you have?"

He ignored it. "You just want her pimp?"

"That's all."

"Harry Falk," Wash said.

"Where can I find him?"

"Got a place on 11th." He thought a moment and gave me a house number. "He's a hippie stud. Attracts a certain kind of girl."

"And both the Barrow girl and the dwarf girl were in his stable?"

He threw a short laugh at me that didn't have any amusement in it. "They *were* his stable. All of it."

"And now he's out of business."

"Unless he's out trying to find somebody to turn out. That takes time. You don't turn a girl out in a weekend."

I sipped at the Bloody Mary. "Why not burn the pimp? Why kill the girls?"

He looked at me like I might be the village idiot. "Shit, a good pimp's hard to find. Cunt's easy."

"So it's just a temporary inconvenience?"

"That's a hard thing to say about those two girls, and I don't intend that. But those are the facts, the hard facts, the economic facts. It's a job of work, turning a girl out right. He's got time and money invested in his girls. And sometimes you miss, and have to write it all off. It turns out the girl's not suited to the life. Time and money down the drain."

"Did you know the Barrow girl?" I'd had my limit of pimp philosophy, and I wasn't sure I could take much more. If he kept talking, he was going to convince me they ought to let him in the Junior Chamber of Commerce.

"I talked to her once or twice."

"How'd she seem? Suited to it?"

"Give me a farm girl, any day," Wash said.

"She seem happy?"

"Happy's not a word you use with these girls. Contented might be a better one. Harry took good care of her."

"She ever say anything about her family?"

"That's what threw me a while ago. What you said about her old country daddy." He shrugged his shoulders. "She said she was an orphan."

I nodded at him and pushed my drink away. I got up and walked over to the elevator, and rode down the twenty-five or twenty-six floors to the lobby.

Marcy answered on the third ring.

"Is Hump there?"

"He called a few minutes ago. He said he had a lead."

"He say where?"

"Down on the Strip, I think," Marcy said.

"He give an address?"

"No."

I told her I'd see her later.

"Thank God for TV late movies," she said.

I had trouble finding the address on 11th. It was on the narrow part of 11th, on that side of Peachtree. On that part of the street,

I always have a feeling there's some dealing going on. It's almost always blocked by a double-parked car or two, and some stud is always leaning out of his ear to try to start something with a girl who's just walking past.

It was a duplex, red brick with white trim around the windows and a white door with the paint chipped. The porch light was off so, I fumbled around the edge of the door, looking for a bell. When I didn't find one, I used my knuckles.

"He's not here." It was a girl's thin, reedy voice.

"What?"

"Harry's not here."

"What?"

The door opened a crack, limited by a chain lock. "You deaf or something?"

"Something," I said. "Where's Harry?"

"He's out."

With the back-lighting, I couldn't get a good look at her, but I saw enough. She needed a wash, or at least a dusting off. I put her age at around fifteen or sixteen. The kind of runaway girl the Strip filled up with during the spring and summer. I guess Harry wasn't heartbroken enough to let his business suffer.

"Where?"

"He didn't say."

"Where does he hang out?"

"He didn't tell me," the girl said.

"Which street corner, which bar?"

"Oh, shit," the girl said. "Try the Lighthouse."

The door edged toward me, closing. I put out a hand and held it open a moment longer. "You tell that to the other guy?"

"The big black dude?"

"That's the one," I said.

"I told him the Pizza House on 10th."

"Which one's the truth?"

"I don't know. He just said he was going out."

I released the door and stepped back. The door slammed and the lock thucked into place.

So much for that. I still didn't know what Harry Falk looked like, and I didn't know his usual hangout. There was the whole Strip out there, the topless joints, the wino places and the hippie taverns. It was three hours or so of hide-and-seek, and I didn't feel like doing it. If Hump hadn't been out there ahead of me, I'd have packed it in for the night and come back in the morning. I couldn't do that now, so I drove over to the Lighthouse and made a slow circuit through the parking lot. No sign of Hump's car. I drove on down to 10th and, as soon as I made the turn, I saw Hump's car parked in one of the spaces next to the corner liquor store. There was a space next to Hump's car. I pulled in and was getting out of the car, when an old man ran out of the liquor store, yelling at me. "You see that sign? Parking's for customers only. I can have you towed."

"Who said I wasn't a customer?" I went into the store with him and bought a fifth of gin and a six-pack of bitter lemon. The old man apologized to me all the way back out to my car. After I locked the gin and the tonic away in the trunk, I asked if it was all right if I parked there for a few minutes while I looked for a friend down the street. He said, "Sure," and that I could take my time. He was just uptight about the street freaks. I guess that made me an upright citizen.

I found Hump at a front booth, just inside the entrance to the Pizza House. He was watching the door and just starting on a pizza that must have been the giant size. Mouth full, he nodded at me and I walked over and sat down across from him.

"We seem to be running in the same track," he said after he swallowed.

"Seems so."

"You looking for Harry, too?"

I said I was.

"He was in earlier. Waitress says he'll come by again."

"We could cruise around and look for him," I said.

"That would be a waste of my charm and a five-dollar bill. She's going to nod him out when he comes in."

The waitress came over and I ordered a beer.

"No beer without ordering food," she said.

"I'm going to eat part of his," I said.

I got the beer and a plate and a fork. While I drank it and worried a slice of the pizza around on the plate, Hump told me about his evening among the black pimps. What kept him out of trouble was that two of them remembered him from the days when he'd been playing defensive end at Cleveland. Still, they hadn't liked the questions about the two girls who'd been killed. All he'd been able to find out from them was the name of the pimp who'd turned them out. Beyond that, it was dead air, and all the talk about sports he wanted to make.

I threw in Wash Johnson's hint that somebody might be trying to put the racket on a protection basis.

"That might explain it. I didn't see any iron, but I had a feel for it, like they were carrying it or it was close by."

"Nothing sacred any more. Not even free enterprise."

"And the cost of living is going up all the time."

"Oh, shit, yes," I said.

"Never saw so many Eldorados in my life." Hump broke off a chunk of crust and chewed on it. "Reminded me of something I read about Wilt Chamberlain. Seems he bought a Bentley, didn't want an Eldorado. Says he liked to pick up a girl now and then. Said a girl looked at an Eldorado and always assumed you were a pimp."

Hump looked up. A young hippie guy had just entered. He was standing there, just looking around. He was wearing tan jeans and a fringed buckskin jacket. The beard was neat, trimmed. The hair wasn't. It was long and red, and it was in a kind of electric frizz-out, a white version of an Afro.

The waitress leaned in, as if to take the pizza pan away. "That's Harry," she said in a whisper.

Hump stood up. At that moment, Harry Falk saw Hump. He turned and was out of the door in a leap. Hump got slowed down because he had to get past the waitress. He finally got free and made the door in about two jumps. I stayed behind and settled the check.

Hump was out on the sidewalk, looking in both directions and shaking his head. "I don't know how he did it. He just disappeared."

We wasted half an hour looking around. We tried the Society Page, the topless place across the street, and we looked in a lot of doorways. No sign of him. "I think he must have called home," I said. "Got told two guys were looking for him."

Hump tail-gated me over to the duplex on 11th. Nobody answered the door this time, and there weren't any lights showing. It looked like Harry Falk and his new girl had gone to ground.

We called it a night. Atlanta's a big city, and it wouldn't do much good running in circles.

I told Hump we'd try again in the morning.

# CHAPTER FOUR

The problem with having a girl who slept over some nights during the week was that I'd have to get up around seven and drive her over to her apartment. The weekends were different, and the morning after the hide-and-seek with Harry Falk was a Sunday, one of those times when I won't even get up to piss unless it hurts. Those mornings I'd get up around eleven, and I'd have a cup of coffee and read the sports page while Marcy made light, crisp biscuits from scratch. While the biscuits were baking, she would fry country ham, that dark and heavily-salted kind that you had to be a Southerner to appreciate. I'd seen Northerners try, and they'd looked like they'd just bitten into a salt tablet.

I never tasted country ham without remembering an uncle who cured his own. I'd been a kid then, and I remembered how he'd put those fresh-killed hams in the salt box and cover them with salt. The hams stayed in the salt box two days for each pound ... a twenty-pound ham for forty days. At the end of that time, he'd wipe the hams off and hang them. He coated them with molasses and coarse-ground black pepper, and he'd wait for the molasses to dry. Then he'd fill some large bags with clean hay, and he'd put the bags over the hams, careful so that there was a layer of hay between the ham and the outside of the bag. That was so the flies couldn't get to the hams and lay their eggs in them. After that, he'd leave them hanging and forget about them until at least the Fourth of July. Since he salted the hams in December, those were long months when the hams dried and aged. After the Fourth of July, it was all right to cut one, and he'd take the bag away. The ham would be green and moldy on the outside. He'd scrub this off with a wire brush and dry it off, and then he'd make the first cut. It would be dark and hard, beautiful inside, and with that salty taste you got just from the smell of it.

Hump called about a quarter to twelve, when Marcy was taking the biscuits out of the oven. The chunks of fried ham were on a plate, draining on paper towels.

"We working today, Jim?"

"Right now, I'm starting a third cup of coffee and about to have myself a country ham and homemade biscuit."

"That an invitation?"

"Come on over. We'll worry about earning our money this afternoon."

"I'll be there in fifteen," he said.

I got back to the kitchen, broke open a biscuit and selected a thin chunk of ham. "Hump's coming over."

"When?"

"Be here in fifteen minutes."

"Fifteen minutes?" There was panic in Marcy's voice, and then I realized why. She was bare-assed under one of my long-sleeved shirts.

"Put on some clothes. I can throw some more ham in the skillet."

"Damn you."

After she went in the bedroom, I got out the package of ham and trimmed off the rind and threw another dozen chunks into the skillet. I set those to cooking. Marcy returned a few minutes later, looking polished and shiny, wearing last night's clothes, the ones she'd worn to the Hollywood Bar. She hadn't bothered with make-up, and I could see the wrinkles around her eyes that usually got covered up.

While I ate a few ham-and-biscuits, she made up another dozen or so scratch biscuits and ran them into the oven. She poured herself another cup of coffee and sat across from me and glowered at me. "The next time you invite Hump over, you'd better warn me."

"I thought you liked him."

"I do, but I'm not doing any bare-assed exhibitions for him or anybody else."

"Just for me, huh? That's nice."

"And sometimes I even worry about you," she said.

But by the time Hump arrived she was over it, and we ate all the biscuits, and all the ham, and almost everything else in the kitchen except the paper towels the ham had drained on. At the end of it, Hump stretched his six-foot-six or seven and smiled at Marcy. "Mighty fine," he said.

Marcy couldn't resist a girlish curtsy in return.

We used Hump's car and dropped Marcy off at her apartment. We angled back over to the Strip. It's slow and dead there on Sundays, no bars open, and not much hustling and buying and selling going on. The few people we passed out on the street seemed to be drifting, just looking for a good patch of sun.

Hump parked in the driveway next to the duplex, and we tried the door. No answer. I left him there and went over and tried the door to the other apartment. No one there either, it seemed. I returned to Hump and spent a couple of minutes looking around, seeing if anybody in the nearby houses or apartments were showing any interest in us. I didn't see anybody at the windows or out on the street.

"Can you spring the lock?" I asked Hump.

"I'll try." Hump grabbed the knob with both hands, leaned a shoulder against the door, and then threw a hip into it. The wood was probably rotten. The screws gave, and the lock swung loose. We stepped inside quickly and closed the door behind us.

It smelled of cat shit. That hit us right away. I didn't realize why it seemed so concentrated, until I saw that all the windows were closed tight and the thermostat was set around 68 or 70. I turned the thermostat down to 60 and opened one of the windows a few inches. While I was doing that, Hump left me and opened the door to the bedroom.

A gray mama cat, sagging belly flapping, darted out of the bedroom and skidded to a stop. She looked at me and yowled. She followed me, still fussing at me, to the kitchen, and rubbed against my leg while I opened a can of cheap cat food and spooned some of it out for her. I left her purring away, and went through the living room and into the bedroom.

"Three new kittens in the closet back here," Hump said. "Maybe a day or two old."

"Anything else?"

"Furniture. Must have come with the apartment, or it was too much trouble moving it on short notice."

It was obvious that the move had been made in a hurry. They hadn't bothered with the dirty sheets on the bed and, in one corner of the room, there was a pile of clothes they'd decided not to take with them. In the bathroom there were a couple of dirty towels, dried hard and stiff.

I looked in the closet. Hump had counted right. Three kittens, eyes not open yet. "Nice people," I said. "Just left the cats to starve to death."

"Looks that way." Hump sat on the edge of the bed and emptied out the metal trash can. He poked around in it with the toe of his shoe. From under the Kleenexes and nearly empty bottles of hand lotion and skin cream, he dug out the two halves of the lease form. The rental agency was Charter and Gross, the rent was $110 a month, and there'd been a security deposit of another $110. I put the lease in my pocket and looked around.

"What are we going to do with the cats?" Hump asked.

"Take them home with me, I guess. Until they're weaned, and then it's the Humane Society."

I carried the mama and Hump carried the box with the kittens. Hump put the box in the back seat and I tossed the mama in after them. The mama didn't like the ride much. Nearing my place, I had Hump make a detour and stop by a 7-11 store. I bought half a dozen cans of cat food and a big bag of the dry kind.

I set the cats up in my garage. I left one of the doors cracked, so the mama could come and go as she liked. I found a couple of old bowls and filled one with water and the other with dry food.

Hump met me at the back steps with a bottle of beer. "Big Daddy done all his work?"

"Fuck off," I said.

While we were drinking the beer, the mama came out of the garage and found us. She bypassed Hump and came straight for me. After sniffing at it, she stretched out on my right shoe and purred.

I called Art Maloney later in the afternoon. "I should have told you," I said, "I'm still working on the girl murder thing." I told him about Harry Falk. "Looks like we might have scared him into hiding."

"Why should he be afraid of you?"

"Some rumors say a protection racket's starting up. Don't know the details yet, but it might be the pimps are being shook down."

"Where'd you hear that?"

"A pimp told me."

"Which pimp?" Art demanded.

"A pimp who doesn't want his name known." Then, to shift ground, I told him that Hump had gotten the same nervous feeling talking to some of the black pimps.

"That's a good story, if it's true. I'll check it out."

"Thought you might," I said. "I'd hate to think I knew things that police intelligence didn't."

"And according to the version you're pushing, the killing of the two girls is a warning?"

"That's the way I heard it."

"That could change it," Art said.

"Sorry. Now it can't be swept under the rug and forgotten."

"Watch your mouth," Art said.

I hung up on him.

After Hump left, I spent the twilight breaking up the rest of the ground in my garden plot. I finished it about the time it went full dark. I checked on the mama when I put the spade and the rake away, and then I had a shower and a couple of stiff gin-and-bitter-lemons. I turned in early and slept nine hours, and was still out of bed and moving around while the cool chill was in the morning air.

A bit after nine, Art called. "You in a better temper today?"

"Like I always am."

"I'm unwinding." That meant Art had come off his shift and was getting ready for bed. "I asked around, and nobody believes that dogshit story of yours about the protection racket."

"Nobody?"

"Nobody with any sense." He paused. "The reason I called. The letter we found in the dwarf girl's purse with the A.P.O. number and the name. Turns out he's her brother. He's in the Army, stationed in Berlin. He'll be flying in today to see about the funeral. His name is Edwin Spinks."

"Where can I reach him?"

"I don't know where he'll be staying. He's coming in on an Eastern flight from New York. Arrives at ten-oh-three."

"I'll meet him."

"Let me hear from you," Art said.

I put on a tie and a light jacket. On the way out, I checked on the mama. It was chow time for the kittens. The mama looked at me like she wanted to come out and play, but couldn't I see she was busy?

I reached Hartsfield International a few minutes before ten. I stopped by the passenger service desk and asked them to page Spinks after the flight arrived. I went into the coffee shop and spent the rest of my waiting time trying to get the attention of a waitress. I gave it up and went back to the passenger service desk. At five after, the flight came in, and a few minutes later they paged Edwin Spinks.

He showed up a couple of minutes later, wearing a rumpled Army uniform with corporal's stripes. I put his age just on the other side of twenty. Dark haircut, regulation length, a pasty complexion with a rash of acne on his chin. Up close, I could read the name tag he wore, and I turned and nodded at the girl at the desk.

"Edwin Spinks?"

"Yeah." He lowered the blue suitcase and looked at me.

I explained that the father of the other girl who'd been killed had asked me to look into it.

"You know Carol?"

"I met her one time … that night."

"I haven't seen her in six months, since I went overseas."

"Anybody meeting you?"

He shook his head.

"Let me give you a ride into town."

He picked up his suitcase and followed me out of the terminal and into the parking lot.

On the expressway headed back into town, he lit up a smoke and looked me over. "I don't see how you're involved. You're not a cop, and you're not a private detective."

"It's a favor for a friend."

"And meeting me at the airport?"

"I thought we might talk on the way in," I said.

"Talk about what?"

"You know what Carol was doing for a living?"

His eyes slid away from me and fastened on the road straight ahead. "I knew, and I didn't like it one fucking bit."

"You know Joy Lynn Barrow?"

"The girl she lived with? I met her a time or two. She seemed nice enough, considering the kind of work she was doing."

"You meet Harry Falk?"

"One time. After that, he stayed out of my way."

"You have trouble?" I asked.

"I wanted to kill him, that's what I wanted to do."

"You try?"

"I got him one time, before he got out of the door," Edwin said.

He didn't look the type to push anybody around. "Why? Because he turned your sister out?"

"That, and something else. You saw Carol? You saw how she was?"

I nodded. "You mean ... little ... like she was?"

"A dwarf," he said harshly. "I didn't like Carol being the freak in his string of girls."

I considered that, but I waited on him, not saying anything.

"What kind of guy would want to ... sleep with her? It had to be some kind of sex freak." He snorted. "A man like that, next it would be girls with one leg."

"I can see that."

"Maybe it still would have bothered me if she whored and if she'd been normal. I don't know. But I think I could have accepted it. But being used to cater to freaks, that makes me sick."

I didn't quite believe him, but if that was the way he wanted to try to deal with it, it wasn't my business to argue with him. "You from Atlanta?"

"Richmond, Virginia," he said.

"When did Carol move down?"

"Two years ago."

"What did Carol do at first?"

"She said she was doing office work, but she never said where. I came down about six months ago, to see her before I shipped out, and she was already selling it on the street."

"You know how she met Harry Falk?"

"She never said."

The skyline was in front of us. It was time to worry about selecting an exit ramp. "You want me to drop you at a hotel? You got a reservation?"

"I thought I'd stay at Carol's apartment."

"The one on 11th?"

"I don't know anything about an apartment on 11th," he said. "I'm talking about the one Carol shared with Joy Lynn."

Bingo. That was Bingo. And score one against me for thinking that both the girls shared a one-bedroom duplex with Harry Falk. Write idiot on my grade sheet.

"It's on St. Charles," he said.

It has a shrub and plant-filled courtyard, this U-shaped apartment building on St. Charles, in northeast Atlanta. It had been built back in the old days, when Ponce de Leon had been one of the better residential areas. St. Charles had probably evolved out of that. Now, in the years since, it had become a hybrid street. Old homes, new apartment houses, and wood frame houses that have been cut up into five or six apartments. It's a quiet street, and the huge old trees that line it give it a small-town feeling.

I parked out on the street, and we went through the stone arch and up the garden-like walk. Some of the plants were blooming, but I never was very strong on knowing which flower was which. Along the U-shaped front of the building were a series of indentations which were entrances to blocks of apartments. Abreast of the third indentation on the right, Edwin nodded and we turned in. After a low flight of stairs, there were mail boxes and two doors facing each other across a box-like hall, and another set of stairs going up to the second level.

"Got a key?"

"They used to leave one out." He leaned his suitcase against the wall and squatted in front of the doormat in front of apartment #10. There was no name card on the door. He turned over the mat. On the back was a kind of sewed-on pocket made of old denim. He stuck a finger in the pocket and brought out a key.

He unlocked the door and put the key in his pocket. We went in. It was an ass-backwards kind of an entrance. We seemed to be coming in from the rear of the apartment. We were in a flat and narrow room that was the dining room. To the left and out of sight was the kitchen. Ahead, down a hallway, there was the living room. Midway in the hall, branching off to the right, were the bedrooms and the bath. I looked in the living room first. A big-component hi-fi and a big-screen color TV. A white sectional sofa and a matching shag carpet. A couple of basket chairs and a small bookcase with novels in it that probably came from the Book of the Month Club.

I went into the bedroom nearest the living room. One look in the closet and I knew I was in the wrong one. The dresses wouldn't fit Joy Lynn. Unless they'd have fitted her when she was nine or ten years old.

I passed Edwin, who was standing in the dining room. He'd opened his suitcase on the table. I knew right away I was in the right bedroom this time. There were a couple of framed photos on the dresser. I recognized John Barrow in both of them. Once standing alone, next to a tractor. In the other one he was seated on the porch of a house, next to a pleasant but plain woman with a bony face and large hands. I guess it was just routine, but I always check the closet first. I was backing out of it a few minutes later, having found nothing there but the faint perfume-scent of Joy Lynn, meshed in the dresses and pants suits, when I found Edwin in the doorway. He'd stripped down to his t-shirt and trousers and was carrying a toilet kit.

"If it's all right, I'm going to shave and shower."

"Go ahead." After he left, I went back to the search. Like the closet, the dresser threw me a blank, too. It didn't seem worth the time. I made the first find in the make-up table. It was mainly mirror, but there were two small drawers on each side. In the bottom drawer on the right I found a diary and a small leather address book. I put the address book aside and opened the diary. It fell open to the page entry for February 6, 1973. The date was the only part of it I could read. The top line looked like nonsense to me:

T1Y2DS 4M2H 4D1YT 3THW YM 2R34DP.

Crap and horseshit. A code. I closed the diary and dropped it on the table. I opened the address book to the first page. It was the same. The heading on the first page was underlined.

4HNJ 3STL

So much for that. I checked the drawers on the other side of the make-up table and found a checkbook and a savings account passbook. If Joy Lynn kept her books well, there was $312.67 in the checking account and a balance of exactly $2,500 in savings.

That gave me a second thought. $2,500 wasn't much for a girl in the street trade to have saved. Unless she was a high spender. But there was always I.R.S., and their ways of pinning down how much you'd earned. Savings was one way. So it was pretty likely that no street girl would bank most of her income.

I returned to the closet and checked it again, looking for some kind of hiding place where she could have stored cash. Nothing. I did the same with the dresser, and drew the same blank. The bed was next. I checked between the mattress and the springs, all the way around. I patted the pillows and started away. On a second thought, I went back to the pillows. In the second one, the one nearest the wall, I found a bulky object and shook it out. It was a brown clasp envelope. I opened the clasp and shook the contents out. They were fifties and hundreds only. With just a rough count, I put the total up somewhere between nine and ten thousand dollars. I bunched the bills up and shoved them back into the envelope. I closed the clasp and, taking up the diary and the address book, I went into the living room. I'd seen the telephone over by the sofa. I sat down and dialed Art's number.

"Not asleep yet?"

"Working toward it," he said. "I might make it, if people stopped calling me."

"I found the apartment where the two girls lived. Also found an envelope with a few thousand dollars in it. Probably unreported crotch money."

"Let me have the address," Art said.

I gave it to him and said I'd wait until he arrived before I left. I hung up and, still hearing the shower running in the bathroom, I left the apartment, the door cracked slightly, and hurried out to my car. I locked the diary and the address book in the glove compartment. The shower was still running when I eased my way back into the apartment. I took the brown envelope into the kitchen with me and found a jar of instant. I put on a saucepan of water. Edwin came in a few minutes later, while I was making a cup. I got a second cup and made him one, too.

"It seems … well … odd being in Carol's apartment, the way things are now."

"I can understand that," I said.

"I'm not sure I want to stay here."

"You might not be able to, anyway. The police are on their way over here now, and they might not let you."

"It's just as well."

"The time you stayed here before, did the girls use this apartment for business?"

"No. Carol said this was their hideaway. They didn't want anything here to tie them to the street."

Art showed up a few minutes later. He had red eyes, and there were dark pouches under them. I passed him the envelope, and he looked in to make sure it was money, after all.

"You check the other bedroom?"

I shook my head. I put my cup in the sink and got ready to leave.

"Where now?" Art asked.

"Hump and I are going to look for Harry Falk."

I left him asking Edwin Spinks some of the same questions I'd already asked. In the living room, I called Hump. He said he'd been trying to reach me for an hour or so. I lowered my voice, in case Art might be listening, and said I'd be by his place in a hour.

Part way out to Emory University, I stopped off to make a call at a service station. The call was to Dr. Fred Clemson at the English department. The secretary said Dr. Clemson wasn't expected at his office until about two-thirty. The seminar in early English drama wasn't until three-thirty, and he'd arrive his usual one hour early to drink coffee with the students in his office. She seemed defensive, like she thought I might be a textbook salesman who'd bother Fred. He had that way with women, and I guess I must be the only man in Atlanta who knew what a bad-ass Clemson had been in his youth, back in the World War Two days.

Bridgewater Drive is just a few blocks past the Emory campus. It's a kind of faculty row, the houses not exactly alike, but nothing radical, either. I turned onto it and followed it for a couple of blocks. I coasted to a stop in front of 722. The house was sort of Irish cottage by way of a Hollywood designer's daydreams.

I unlocked the glove compartment and got out the diary and address book. I didn't bother with the front door. I walked up the driveway instead, and reached the left rear corner of his house. His study was there. The drapes were drawn, but I could see light past a break in the center seam. I reached up and rapped on the window.

The irritation faded from his face when he recognized me. He grinned and pointed toward the back of the house, where the rear entrance was. By the time I got there, the door was open and he was waving me inside.

"Jim, dammit, come on in here."

"Don't mean to interrupt," I said. "The secretary said you have a seminar this afternoon."

"I have plenty of time." He led me down a narrow hallway to his study. "I assume you have some problem."

The way he said it, I knew if I hadn't had a problem it would have ruined his day. Fred's tall and thin and graying now, and scholarly to the nth degree, but back in the 1940's he'd been a real hotshot in Naval intelligence with a specialty in codes. Somehow, after those days, the picky shit with scholarship must be a bit of a comedown.

"A small one," I said. I passed the diary to him. It was probably the way the book was bound or the back was broken. Anyway, it opened to the same entry I'd puzzled over when I'd first found it, the one for February 6.

"Ah ..." Holding the diary in one hand, he used the other hand to clear a space on his overloaded desk. He sat down and I stood behind him and looked over his shoulder. He stared down at the diary entry for a few moments, then turned and grinned at me. "It's a cipher that a child might have made up. You remember the coded messages on the wrapper ends of Merita Bread, back in the 1940's?"

I did. Merita Bread had sponsored the Lone Ranger on radio back then, and after you sent off for the decoding ring, you could work out the secret messages hidden on the wrapper. It always turned out to be something on the moral side. "Obey your mother" or "Cross the street only with the green light."

"There are two things you can do with the plain text ... the message. You can work out some way of transposing the letters, jumbling them so they don't seem to mean anything, or you can devise some method of substitution. That is, a certain letter or number stands for another letter."

"Which is it?"

"It's a simple combination of both," he said. He drew a legal pad toward him and flipped over a few pages to find a clean sheet. He wrote down the top line of the February 6 entry.

T1Y2DS 4M2H 4D1YT 3THW YM 2R34DP.

"Notice the fifth word over ... the ym? It's a dead giveaway. It shows how the transposition works. If the person who wrote this was a bit brighter, he or she would have devised some way of eliminating two-letter words. Just left them out completely. As it is, the fifth word is *my*, and it shows us that we're working with a code where the first letter of each word is moved to the end of the word." He dug under a pile of papers and found a pack of smokes. He lit one and blew the smoke up at me. "The person who wrote this diary ... would you say they hoped it would stand up against some kind of professional scrutiny? Or is it just to keep the casual peeper away?"

"The casual peeper, I'd think." I took a minute and filled him in on Joy Lynn, and how she'd died.

"So it's just to keep a pimp or a roommate from getting their curiosity satisfied?"

"My guess."

"There are no vowels showing. We do have numbers…in this line 1, 2, 3 and 4." He pointed to a line below. "And a 5 here. Five vowels and five numerals used. There are ways they could be shifted around, or they could be used straight. These look straight to me. Just a straight substitution. And that makes sense. With something like this, she'd want to write it out with as little trouble as possible. She wouldn't want to have to keep referring to a code sheet. That's why the transposition is so simple. Now, let's try the straight-down-the-line numeral-for-vowel substitution."

He wrote down T1Y2DS. "Let's shift the s back to the beginning of the word, let's assume the 1 is a substitution for the first vowel, a, the 2 for the vowel e, and we have the first word, *stayed.*"

His pen darted over the page. He translated the first line in a matter of seconds. *Stayed home today with my period.*

"The hooker's day off," I said.

"You want me to translate some more?"

"A waste of your time." But on second thought, I reached in my coat pocket and got out the address book. "Does this use the same code?"

He opened it to the first page. "The same." He wrote down the heading, which was underlined. 4HNJ 3STL. "John List. What does that mean?"

"You are an innocent," I said. "It's how the hooker gets off the street. She puts together a list of steady customers. And when the list is long enough, she just puts her ass in the chair next to the phone and services the ones from the list and any new ones who get recommended to her. No more being hassled by cops, or hanging around street corners."

Fred put the diary and the address book together and handed them to me. "Next time, I hope it'll be a more complex code."

"I'll do my best."

He followed me to the back door. "Of course, if you think there are going to be some juicy parts, I'll run off a decoding for you."

"I think it'll be dull, dull, dull," I said.

He was shaking his head sadly while I thanked him. He was still in the doorway when I rounded the corner of the house and headed down the driveway to my car.

Hump and I spent the afternoon on the Strip. If Harry Falk was still around he was well hidden, or nobody wanted to make a few bucks telling us where he was. Around five, we called it an afternoon and decided we'd try again later, when the nightcrawlers came out.

After I dropped Hump, I stopped by a Kroger's and bought some salad things, some charcoal and lighter, a couple of steaks, and a few cans of cat food. At a wine store down the street, I bought a reasonable bottle of *Beaujolais*.

I drove over to Marcy's apartment and sat in the car, in the parking lot, until Marcy drove up. I kidnapped her right on the spot and drove straight over to my house. Marcy played with the gray mama cat and the kittens, and then she went in and started making the salad. I was out in the yard, sweeping the spider webs from the grill and trying not to step on the mama cat, who was underfoot when the phone rang.

Marcy took the call and yelled at me from the back door.

Art was on the line. "You have any luck with Harry Falk today?"

"Not a bit."

"I might have something," he said. "A crew from the city parks department was working over at the lake in Piedmont Park. They were out in a boat, putting out the ropes that mark off the area where the little kids swim. They think they sighted a body on the bottom. I'm headed that way now. You know what Falk looks like. It might be worth a look."

I said I'd be there about the time he was.

Before I left, I got out the diary and told Marcy that de-coding it was a lot more educational than watching TV. She was working over the first entry when I left and headed for Piedmont Park.

# CHAPTER FIVE

The Piedmont Park lake is artificial. It was created for the 1895 Cotton States Exposition, which had a bit of everything, including President Cleveland and Buffalo Bill and his Wild West Show. After the Exposition there was some serious haggling about the value of the land, but in the end, quite a bit of it was set aside as a park. Now there are baseball fields, tennis courts, greenhouses, a golf course and the lake.

I found Art seated on a bench at the edge of the lake. He nodded and patted the empty half of the bench to his right. "The envelope from the Barrow girl's room had $8,950 in it."

"You find one in the dwarf girl's room?"

"It had $6,400 in it."

I looked out toward the lake. There was a rowboat out in the middle of it. One swimmer in trunks and a tank-suit top manned it, leaning over the side of the boat and staring down into the water. Now and then a face, masked by scuba gear, would pop up, remain on the surface for a few moments, and then tip over and dive out of sight. All around the fringes of the lake, back from the roadblocks the police had set up, people were watching the drama in the center of the lake. It was probably better than going home and getting ready for an evening of reruns on the TV.

"What happens to the money?" I asked.

"I.R.S. will be interested. So will the state. What's left might end up in the estates." Art cut his eyes toward me. "You help yourself to any of it?"

"Wish I had." I shook my head. "I'm being paid."

"But tempted?"

"A bit." I nodded out in the direction of the rowboat and the divers. "What makes you think this might be Falk?"

"A guess. He dropped out of sight a little too well."

"And a day or so after his stable got butchered. It figures."

"Still, it's a long shot," Art said. He stood up. "I think the divers have it."

Near the rowboat, two heads were out of the water now. Between them they appeared to be supporting something large and awkward. In the next five minutes, they tried a couple of times to get the object into the rowboat. Each time, the boat came close to capsizing. After the second attempt, one of the divers waved the rowboat away. The oars biting in deep, the boat moved ahead of the divers toward the lake's edge, where we were. The two divers followed and, as they got closer, I could hear their grunts of exertion. The boat arrived at the grassy ledge first, and Art walked over and talked to the swimmer who manned it. From my position at the bench, I couldn't hear what they were saying.

Art came back to the bench, shaking his head. "It might not be Falk, after all. He says it's two bodies, a guy and a girl."

"How …?"

"Tied together."

As the divers neared the shore, Art moved toward them, and this time I followed. The two attendants from the meat wagon hurried over and motioned me out of the way, so they could spread the tarp. The divers, breath rasping now, pulled the bodies to the front edge of the tarp and stood there, bent over and gagging. The meat wagon attendants took over then and pulled the bodies the rest of the way.

It was Shakespeare's beast with the two backs. Both bodies were naked. They'd been tied together face to face and groin to groin, using a heavy nylon cord. I could see the water-washed and puckered bullet holes in both of them. It looked like somebody had used about half a box of shells on them. I couldn't believe they'd been that hard to kill.

"Jim," Art said.

I stepped onto the tarp. It crackled under my feet. The way they were positioned, the girl on top, I couldn't get a good look at the man. I leaned this way and that. Finally, an impatient attendant grabbed the girl by the hair and pulled her head to the side. I got my long look then, and at the same time I had a few moments to peer at the girl.

I straightened up. "I think it's Falk," I said, "but that's on the basis of a short look at him at the Pizza House."

Art met me at the edge of the tarp. "And the girl?"

"That makes it more than a guess. I had a longer look at her. I think she's the girl who was at Falk's place Saturday night. Probably going to be part of his new stable."

Flash bulbs cracked behind me. I didn't look around.

"Getting rough," Art said. "Two hookers, one pimp and one possible apprentice."

"The rumor making more sense now?"

"I'm still fighting it," Art said.

I looked back, out at the lake. "How'd they get out there?"

"The rowboat. The people from Parks found the chain cut. At first, they just assumed some freaks did it, so they could joy ride on the lake when the park was closed."

"But no way to know whether they were dropped in early Sunday morning or early this morning?"

"Not until the medical examiner does his work."

I forced myself to turn and look at the bodies on the tarp. The photographer had finished, and now they were cutting the nylon cord and prying the bodies apart. "It's obscene," I said. "Especially if it's just a warning. Pay your union dues, or this happens."

"If it's that," Art said. "I've got a stop to make. You want to tag along?"

"Where?"

"I found out Falk has a wife ... a widow now. Might as well see if she knows anything."

I shook my head. "I've seen enough of the Falks for one day."

"Is that all of it?"

"I've got two steaks, and the charcoal's not even lit yet."

"Marcy?"

I nodded. "Getting hungry and mean."

I got the charcoal lit and went into the kitchen. From inside the kitchen, I tried the light over the back steps. It was still working. That meant I wouldn't have to do the cooking in the dark. Marcy was at the kitchen table, bent over the diary and a pad of writing paper she'd found somewhere.

"How's it going?"

"It's getting easier." Marcy looked up. "But I don't think I'd want to do this for a living."

I got out the cork puller and eased the cork out of the *Beaujolais*. "When does the diary start?"

"July of last year."

I found the two wine glasses where she'd put them, and poured us each a half glass. I sat down at the table across from her and read what she'd decoded so far:

*July 7, 1972:I didn't want to go tonight and Harry got mad with me. He says he loves me but he is not going to put up with the way I am acting. First we had a big fight and screamed and yelled and then we made love. He told me no matter what I thought I was his bottom woman and after a few more months we would have enough money to go to Spain and live there for two or three years just like rich people.*

*I want to believe him but it is hard. Afterwards I got dressed and he dropped me on the corner of North Avenue and Peachtree.*

*I tricked ten times and made three hundred but I told him seven times and held back ninety dollars. That is just in case he is lying to me.*

*It was after three when I got home.*

When I turned the page over, I looked up and saw Marcy watching me. She took the page and looked at it. "Jim? What's a bottom woman?"

"It means the main woman. A pimp might have three or four or five girls working for him, and he might be screwing all of them to keep them happy. But usually he's got his strongest tie with one of them. That's his bottom woman."

"So it's part of the con?"

"It could be the truth." But I wasn't really thinking about the conversation about a bottom woman. I was thinking about the almost $9,000 in the envelope in Joy Lynn's pillow. If she was putting aside $90 a night, and had been for nine or ten months, $9,000 sounded a little light. Of course, maybe it wasn't that much each working night. But I made a note to myself to run a total of the. amounts she'd squirreled away. And I realized that this squirreling away and writing it down was one good reason for keeping the diary in code. I'd heard of some pretty nasty things that pimps had done when they'd found out one of their girls was holding back on them.

Marcy smiled over the edge of her wine glass. "Am I your bottom woman, Jim?"

"Bottom and top," I said.

I went on to the second entry she'd decoded.

*July 8,1972: Boy am I mad today. About the time I got up Harry brought over a new girl. Her name is Crystal Hanner. Her hair is blonde but I do not think it is the real color. Harry said from now on Crystal is going to share the apartment with me and sleep in the spare room. Harry saw I didn't like it and he followed me into the bedroom and closed the door. He said he didn't like taking on a second girl either but we just were not making money as fast as he wanted to. With Crystal hustling too we could get to Spain faster and we could stay longer.*

*I still do not like it. For one thing we will be paired together and it will be harder for me to lie about the number of tricks I do each night. And if I hold money back and she does not it will seem that she is doing better than I am out on the street.*

*I hustled while he helped her move her things in. I was mad because I knew that he was doing a lot more than just helping her move her clothes in.*

*I tricked nine times and told him seven. I held back sixty dollars and he was mad with me and said I must not have been trying very hard.*

I turned the page over and looked at Marcy. "This all you've done so far?" I grinned at her. "You must not be trying very hard."

"You think it's easy, you do some," she said.

I got up. "Not me. Got to check on the charcoal."

I went outside and looked at the coals. They weren't anywhere near ready, and I'd known it. I sat on the steps and sipped my wine. The mama cat trotted over and rubbed against my leg. I scratched her behind the ears and listened to the purring that brought on.

Back during my days on the force, when I'd just been starting out, I had done some time on vice. You'd act like a nerd and let the girl solicit you, and then you'd go to her room, and when she took the money, you arrested her. Back then, I don't think prostitution was that big a business. But now, the town was growing at a hell of a rate. Exploding. Trying to become a big convention city. And that meant heading toward Hooker City, U.S.A.

I thought of the two days in the life of Joy Lynn Barrow, the ones Marcy had just decoded. Sociologists and forward-thinking policemen like to think of prostitution as one of the victimless crimes. Maybe so. But Joy Lynn seemed to be a victim to me. But, then, I guess it depends upon your definition of a victim.

❧    ❧    ❧

Marcy finished another page before I put on the steaks. It wasn't much new. Joy Lynn and Crystal weren't getting along too well, and Joy Lynn thought Crystal was using her shampoo, and she didn't like using the toilet without spraying the seat with Lysol spray. And with Crystal paired off with her, it was hard to hide the number of tricks she turned. On this night, because she wanted to bring home as much money as Crystal, she'd only put by $30.

I got the steaks the way both of us liked them, charred on the outside and bloody under the crust. We had just salad and the rest of the wine with it.

Marcy said she was tired, and I dropped her after she did the dishes. She took the diary with her and said she'd translate as much as she could, using her lunch hour and her breaks. She didn't say so, but I had a feeling she was intrigued with this look into the gutter life.

Art called a few minutes after I got back. Harry Falk's widow had made a positive ID on the body. Beyond that, she didn't have much to say, except for the fact that she hated him.

On impulse, I mentioned that I'd heard the name of another girl who'd been part of Falk's stable some months back.

"You say Crystal Hanner? Hold a minute."

He was off the line for a couple of minutes. When he came back, he said, "She's one of the well-known ones. She's got a long record of arrests."

"You got an address?"

"Better than that," Art said. "We're in luck. She's in the slam right now."

"For what?"

"Same thing. Selling her ass."

"I'd like to talk to her," I said.

"Why?"

"God knows. It might be so long ago, she might not know anything worth going to the trouble for."

"I'll call you back. Let me see what I can arrange."

As soon as Art was off the line, I called Hump. I'd called him after my return from the lake. With Harry Falk dead, it looked like all the roads were closed. They'd all turned dead-end. And I had a feeling that if this was a racket-involved kill, I was going at it all wrong. I was under some stupid compulsion to put together a biography of Joy Lynn. And it was a million-to-one against me knowing who'd killed her, even after I knew everything else about her, if I stayed on the same track.

"Hump," I said, "you might have a night off."

"I don't need a night off."

I told him I might be going out to talk to a hooker who'd known the Barrow girl some months back. "That grab you?"

"Might be worth a listen."

I said I'd call him after I'd talked to Art.

"It took some talking, but I sprung her. I argued the chance of the protection racket, and needing an informant out on the street."

"She buy your deal?"

"Says she does."

"Where do I meet you?"

He said Crystal wanted to shower and change clothes after a day in the slam. She lived in the Central Hotel, on Courtland, and he'd drop her there and wait for me at the Book Store Bar, a place about half a block from the hotel. Crystal would meet us there after she'd cleaned herself up.

"You mind if I bring Hump?"

"You ever go anywhere without your shadow?"

I said I didn't, and he said to bring him along.

The Book Store Bar was a strange idea gone even stranger. There were bookcases all along the walls, and they were filled with real books. The story I'd heard was that on opening day, they'd given a free drink for every two hardback books brought in. They'd filled the shelves in one afternoon, but most of them seemed to be old, out-of-date college textbooks.

Even before our first drink arrived, Art was on me. "How'd you hear about Crystal Hanner?"

"Around," I said.

"You know something, you better let me know."

"That's all I know right now." There was a certain amount of truth in that. I wouldn't know any more until Marcy decoded some more pages. But I knew Art would love to get his hands on Joy Lynn's john list even more than the diary. He'd probably get it, in time. Cops like to think that most violent deaths are the result of passion, and the john list would give Art the names of some men in her life. He'd put blinders on until he checked them out. The blinders were so he wouldn't allow himself to know that most crimes of passion weren't committed that way, like some scene out of an early James Cagney flick.

I'd have some tall lying to do when I turned the diary and the address book over to him.

Hump took the heat off me. He started talking about the Braves and Hank Aaron. Even with his mind on other things, Art couldn't resist the chance to badmouth the Braves. From that, they moved on to an estimate of how many games the Braves would win the whole season. They were haggling around sixty games. I wasn't paying much attention. I was looking around the bar, feeling better, off the sharp hook.

It was then that I saw the four of them. They came in with the precision of a Vince Lombardi end sweep. They didn't fit the

Book Store Bar. They belonged in Vegas. Big city muscle. Not the type for knives or guns. Maybe a blackjack or two.

I dropped a hand under the table and gave Hump a tap on the knee. He didn't break stride, kept on talking about how Aaron didn't like to play first base, but his head turned to follow my eyes and register the muscle. He must have passed the tap on to Art. For now his head went around easy and slow.

Two of the four peeled off and fitted themselves into a space near the center of the bar, to our left and not far away. The remaining two stood in the doorway for a count of about ten, eyes moving around the large room, searching. When their gaze reached our table, I saw a hesitant flicker and a skip on past.

"Who are they looking for? You know either of those two?"

Hump shook his head, his answer to Art's questions.

"I think we've been jobbed," I said.

"The girl?"

"My guess." Damn her. "You carrying, Art?"

Art said he was. "But I can't pull iron in a crowded room like this."

I tipped my head at Hump. "It's time you finished your talk with us and went back to your place at the bar. Shake hands, like a polite boy."

"That wouldn't fool my grandmama." But Hump pushed back his chair, smiling, and shook each of us by the hand. He lifted his drink and carried it over to the bar. When he pushed in next to the two hard-asses he planted himself toward the lower end of the bar, putting himself between them and the table where Art and I were.

The two near the entrance watched the charade with the handshaking and wanted to believe it, but I don't think they could. Hump was the unknown, and they didn't like the setup when they couldn't predict it. They were worrying it around in their heads, not liking it. Still, they'd set it in motion, and I guess they decided to play it out.

They made their move. The two near the door stepped out, moving single-file down the aisle between the tables. They stopped about a foot or so from our table and looked at us. They were both about the same size, two hundred or a bit past that. The one who paired off with me had the shoulders and arms for wrestling bears, and a face with deep acne craters about the size of tack heads spread across his cheeks. The other one, the one facing Art, wasn't marked. In fact, now that he was close enough, I could see that he didn't match the mold the others were taken from. He was about forty, with a salting of gray hair. He looked like someone who might sell you insurance any night on national TV. But not the eyes. The eyes wouldn't sell you anything but death. They were the eyes of a man three days dead.

"You're Art Maloney," the one with the dead eyes said.

"That's me."

"We've got a friend in common."

"I doubt that," Art said.

"You sent him up a couple of years ago."

"That explains it," Art said. "He was no friend of mine."

"I told him I was passing through Atlanta, and he said for me to be sure and look you up."

"What's his name?"

"Names don't matter."

"All right, all this horseshit aside," Art said, "what is it you want?"

"Don't rush it. There's plenty of time." He turned his head slowly and looked at Hump. "Who's the big spade?"

"Ask him that way and he'll tell you," I said.

He'd been ignoring me. Now his eyes swept back from the bar and locked on me. "Jim Hardman, ex-crooked cop." He smiled at me. "Or is it Jim Hardman, crooked ex-cop?"

"Why the names? You got to list us on your expense account?"

"That's not bad," he said. He nodded to the bruiser squared off against me. "He's making a joke, Frank."

"Is that a joke?" Frank's voice cracked. It sounded like somebody'd almost ripped his throat out one time or another.

"In some circles," I said.

All the talking wasn't getting us anywhere. They'd come to beat on us, and nothing was going to change that. If they'd come to warn us off, they'd have done it and gone on their way. The element that was holding them back was the unknown, Hump. They'd come four against two, and found it might be four against three. Now they were probably wishing they'd brought six.

I slid my near shoe across the carpet and tapped Art on the ankle. That meant heads up, it is about to happen.

At the bar, Hump planted his left elbow on the padded rail and gave me a questioning look. I nodded and set it off.

Hump whirled and hit the stud next to him as hard as he could, getting all his weight into it. I could hear the splat over the low music. The splat and the grunt that went with it startled the two in front of us, but I knew it wouldn't last long. I braced my feet under me and pushed the table toward the bruiser, Frank. He caught it in his hands and grinned at me. The grin said he was going to do terrible things to me. But as I came out of the chair, I reached behind me and caught the chair by the top rung and swung it toward him. He was pushing the table away from him when I stepped around it and hit him about hip-high with the chair. The shock almost tore it out of my hands. It wasn't a break-away chair, like in the flicks, and if it broke anything, it might have been a bone in Frank's hip. It hurt him, and he grunted with the pain. But his hands were free now, with the table pushed away, and he brought up the hands. I could see a busted knuckle or two, and I swung the chair again. I aimed lower this time, and I had to move under a right he was throwing. It was ticketed for my face, but I bent under and felt it rip across the top of my head. That shook me some, and I could feel my knees give. The chair reached him and banged him across the knees. With any luck, there went a cracked kneecap. He grabbed the chair and pulled at it, and I held on and pulled against him, and then turned it loose. That fooled him, and he was falling back, hands full of the chair, when I stepped in close and hit him as hard as I could in the neck. It stunned him and his head bent back, mouth open, gasping for breath. His throat was open, unprotected, and I put the same fist in the soft part of it. He went down, holding his throat with both hands, like I'd broken up the rest of it, and rolled on his side, retching and vomiting.

I stepped around him and looked for Art. The one fronting Art hadn't lost his reflexes, like mine had. He had Art backed up against one of the big bookcases, and books were thudding off onto the floor. Art was giving as good as he was getting, but it was too close to an even fight, and it might take time for one or the other to wear down. I didn't feel like waiting that long. I stopped behind the stud with the dead eyes and hit him in the right kidney. The breath went out of him like a whistle with a scream buried under it. I left the rest of it to Art, and turned to the bar.

It was under control there. One of the studs was on the floor next to the bar. That was probably the first one Hump had hit. The other one had made more of a fight of it. They'd fought their way down the length of the room, through the crowd, toward the front door. Hump had taken it out of him, finally. When I reached them, Hump had him by the neck, backed against the wall near the cigarette machine, up on his tiptoes. Blood ran out of both nostrils and out of the torn bottom lip.

The bartender was nervous. "I called the police."

I nodded toward Art. "He's police himself." There was plenty of room at the bar. I pointed at the J&B. He poured me a stiff one. I knocked it back. I pushed the glass back at him. "This time, on the rocks." While he poured, I could hear the sirens. I ran a hand over the top of my head. No blood, but I was going to have a knot in an hour or so. I carried the J&B on the rocks down to Hump. Hump opened the balled fist he'd been threatening the guy with and took the glass. "Now you're not going to bother me while I'm drinking, are you?"

The stud shook his head. The blood ran down the side of his neck. Hump nodded and gulped at his drink.

A couple of minutes later, two police cruisers arrived. As soon as Art had it explained to them and I could move away from the bar, I went into the bathroom to wash my face. I was bent over, scooping water by the handful, when I felt the last drink of scotch come choking back up. I let it gush into the sink, and then I went on washing my face.

I didn't feel too bad about the scotch. I hadn't paid for it.

# CHAPTER SIX

"She went out right after she got here," the desk clerk at the Central Hotel said.

"Any phone calls?" Art asked.

"Not through the switchboard." The desk clerk was in his early thirties. The way he dressed and carried himself showed that he fancied himself a bit. Now, as if he was in a stage play, he turned and looked at the bank of pay phones against one wall of the grimy lobby.

"You see her make a call?"

"I didn't see anything." He also had the cheap-hotel sickness, the one that made you blind and deaf.

Art put out his hand. "The key to her room."

"You got a search warrant?"

"I don't need one." Art kept his palm out, waiting.

"I'm not supposed to do that."

"I've had a bad night," Art said. "If you don't put that key in my hand in about five seconds, I'm going to come around there and stomp your ass, and *then* I'm going to charge you with assaulting an officer, and *then* I'm going to take that key and go up to her room."

The room key hit his palm a split second later.

Hump remained behind in the lobby while we took the self-service elevator up to the fifth floor. "I'm going to have a hell of a time explaining what happened to my new informant," Art said.

"It tells us one thing," I said. "She's more afraid of them ... whoever they are ... than she is of the police."

"I should have camped outside her door," Art said.

"No way you could have known."

The elevator doors opened. We passed a beverage dispenser, a cigarette machine, and a candy and snack-cracker machine. It looked like the Central Hotel didn't do much in the way of room service, unless you ordered a hooker.

A wrinkled pants suit was thrown across the bed in room 508, along with some sweat-dirty underwear and a pair of stockings. While Art checked around the room, I went into the bathroom. The tub was bone dry. A washcloth on the shower curtain railing was damp. Crystal Hanner had been in a hurry. She'd settled for what we used to call a Marine bath. That's a quick dab under the armpits with a wash cloth and a splash of shaving lotion ... or, in her case, cologne or perfume.

"Nothing," I said, going back into the bedroom.

Art turned from some clothes in the closet. "Wears expensive clothes. Better than Edna does."

"Yeah," I said, "but she has to let a lot of strangers stick their clap stick in her, to afford them."

"You through?"

I nodded, and we rode the elevator back down to the lobby. The desk clerk had his nerve back. I guess he'd been pumping and puffing it up while we were upstairs.

"I'm going to call the hotel's lawyer first thing in the morning. You can't just run over people this way."

"Do it." Art slapped the key down on the desk.

I put an elbow on the counter and gave him my kindest smile. "Do it, but know the rotten can of peas you're opening. You're running close to a cathouse here. The police have all the time in the world. They'll take five years proving it if they have to."

"The Hanner girl," Art said. "She leave in a cab, or did somebody pick her up?"

"I didn't see," the clerk said.

"Do better than that," Art said.

He choked again. "In a cab."

"Which kind?"

"Terminal City," the clerk said.

We went out to the street. It was cool and the wind was up. It was like this in the early spring. There was a trace of dampness in the air, like it might rain. It made me think about my vegetable garden. I was going to have to get some seeds in soon. Otherwise, I was going to be pissed every time it rained for the next week or two.

"I'll trace her through the cab company," Art said.

"It'll lead you to a street corner or the bus station."

"Got to try it, anyway."

I dropped Hump off and went on home. In my bathroom mirror, I checked the knot on top of my head. The skin wasn't broken, but it was stretching some now. I talked myself out of a drink and got into bed, trying to dive into sleep past the beginning of a headache.

In the morning, the knot was there, but it didn't look as large as it felt. I sat around the kitchen until eight, reading the paper and drinking coffee. At exactly eight, knowing it was time for Marcy to leave for work at the welfare department, I dialed her number.

"I knew it would be you," Marcy said. "And all you want is to know how many more pages I've decoded."

"Not exactly." I liked it when she misjudged me. "I wondered if you could find the time to pick up some seeds for me?"

"What do you need?"

"Summer squash, corn. Anything else you like."

"Zucchini," she said.

"We can do a few hills of each, summer and zucchini."

"I'll try."

"And keep on translating," I said.

After she said she loved me, too, I made another cup of coffee and carried it out into the backyard. It had rained during the night, while I was sleeping, but it hadn't been a heavy rain. The ground wasn't soggy. I leaned on the terrace wall and drank the coffee and felt the coolness after the rain. The spring was really getting cranked up. You could almost hear the leaf buds breaking open.

So much for the spring. My look into the death of Joy Lynn wasn't going too well. It was down the dark tunnel and the dead-end waiting. The four muscle men from the night before weren't going to say anything. I'd heard them rehearsing-it with the cops, right after they arrived at the Book Store Bar. It was just a barroom argument that got out of hand. And, of course, they'd made a lot of the fact that Hump had thrown the first punch. Even if a judge believed Art, it would be a short time in the slam. And because they were pros, they'd take the soft time and be back on the street, still in good shape with whoever had sent them, and maybe with a bonus for taking the fall with their mouths closed.

Crystal Hanner might know something. No doubt at all, she'd put the ugly four on us. Or she'd called somebody who'd put them on us. A talk with her, if Art could locate her, might send us off in a new direction.

I carried my empty coffee cup back into the kitchen. I was thinking of calling Art, when he called me.

"That's good mind-reading," I said.

"About to call me?"

"Hand on the phone," I said.

"I located the driver, the one who picked up somebody at the Central Hotel about the right time. The problem is, he called in right after that and wrote himself off for the rest of the night. I got his address and his phone number, but I can't reach him."

"Sounds like the right one," I said.

"Name's Freddie Black." He read me off an address on Monroe Drive. "I think it's one of those wood frame apartment houses near where Monroe and Ponce de Leon come together."

"You want me to check it?"

"If you want to," Art said. "I'm bushed. I need a few hours of sleep."

"What if I turn up something?"

"Give me two hours sleep, and then call me."

I said I would. I dialed Hump's number. He sounded awake. I guess he'd gone straight to bed after I'd dropped him. "I'm going looking for a cab driver."

"I need my breakfast."

"Check with you later, then," I said.

"No, wait. It shouldn't take long to peel the driver down. After that, we get some breakfast."

"Done," I said.

Hump was parked in a side street that faced the Monroe address. He honked at me as I went by. I got the car turned around and went into the street and parked behind him.

"No sign of the cab," Hump said.

I leaned on the open car window and looked over at the house. "I'm not sure about the Terminal City Cab Company, whether they lease by the week and let the driver keep the cab full-time, or the other way."

"Let's try it," Hump said.

We crossed Monroe Drive. It was a big wood frame house with a tin roof. It had been painted a battleship gray, maybe with surplus paint, back in the summer. The floor boards on the porch didn't look too safe. I picked my way across the porch to the rack of mailboxes. Next to the mailboxes, facing out to the street, was a hand-lettered sign that announced there was a furnished apartment for rent. ADULTS ONLY—NO PETS.

By the number of mailboxes, there were six apartments. An F. Black had apartment #4. I pushed into the hallway. Apartments 1 and 2 faced each other across a boxlike hallway. There was a staircase straight ahead. We went up to the second floor. I found #4, but I couldn't find a bell. I rapped on the door panel. When there wasn't an answer, I tried again.

The door across the hall cracked open a few inches. "He's not home," a woman said.

"He come in last night?"

"No," she said.

"Do you know …?"

The door jerked open a few more inches, and I could see a woman in her forties, heir hair up in tissue and curlers. "All I know is, I've got a headache and you're not helping it any."

"One question, and we'll leave your headache alone. Does he keep the cab while he's off duty?"

"Sure. It's parked out in the driveway. Makes the house took cheap, I think."

"Thanks."

"Breakfast?" Hump asked when we reached his car.

"Breakfast," I said.

I locked my car, and we drove down Ponce de Leon until we reached Mrs. Pearson's Cafe. The sign out front was in the shape of a big puffy homemade biscuit. That was the specialty of the place, served with butter and honey. I ordered coffee and a couple of sausage biscuits. While I ate those, I watched Hump work through six eggs, a couple of orders of bacon, and about a dozen hot biscuits. It bloated me, watching him.

"How's the decoding going?" Hump asked, catching his breath over a second cup of coffee.

"It might take some time."

"You doing anything with the john list?"

"Not so far. I don't think it'll lead us anywhere. Why?"

Hump shook his head.

I caught the check. Hump left the tip. Hump's breakfast was almost a lunch tab downtown. Hump held the door open and grinned at the change I got from a five-dollar bill.

At eleven-thirty or so, the cab made its turn into the driveway and parked. I tapped Hump on the shoulder, and we left his car

PIMP FOR THE DEAD

and went across the street at a fast walk. Black was checking his mailbox when we reached the steps.

"You Freddie Black?"

"What if I am?"

Black was a short, feisty man in his mid-twenties. He was wearing a windbreaker, so I couldn't be sure, but he looked the type to have tattoos on both arms and his chest. Right now, he needed a shave.

"We're interested in a girl you picked up in front of the Central Hotel last night. Your last trip."

"What's she to you?"

"You make any guess about her profession?" I asked.

He nodded.

"That girl rolled me, not half an hour before you picked her up." I looked down at the ground like it wasn't that easy to tell strangers what a fool I'd been, "I made a complaint at the police. A detective named Art Maloney's been looking for you all night."

He bought it. "How much she roll you for?"

"Close to five hundred," I said.

"No wonder she was in a big hurry."

"Where'd you take her?"

"She gave me twenty above the fare so I wouldn't say."

"You've still got the twenty, and I won't tell her I got anything from you."

"I took her to the bus station," he said.

"Not a chance," I said. "You've been gone all night. Maybe you didn't drive her to South Carolina or Florida, but it was a long trip." I gave him a long look up and down. "My guess is, you took a nap on the side of the road."

"This won't get back to the cab company?"

"No way," I said. I could see him relaxing, getting ready. "And I'll call the cop and keep him off your back."

"You know a town named Fletcherville, near the Carolina line?"

"Yeah." It wasn't on the main route north. It was more westerly. I hadn't been there, but I'd heard of it. It was about a three-hour drive. "Three hours to get there. That would put you there around midnight."

"Later," Black said. "We stopped for supper."

"Where'd you drop her in Fletcherville?"

"That was the odd part. She had me leave her right on the main street."

"Anything open, that time of night?"

"Maybe a cafe and the hotel," he said. "It's the kind of town where it's locked up tight at nine or ten."

"You see her head for the cafe or the hotel?"

"Not while I was watching her. She was just standing there, with that little overnight case."

"You nap on the road?"

"The money I made last night, I stopped in the first motel I saw." Then the thought hit him, and he didn't like it. "I guess she paid me with your money."

"Forget it," I said. "You didn't have any way of knowing it was stolen."

Hump and I started away.

"You'll keep your word about the cab company?"

I said I would.

At twelve-thirty I called Art, and had to fight my way past his wife, Edna. She didn't want to wake him up. We'd been friends for a long time, but she wanted Art to get his seven or eight, no matter how important the business was.

Art drove over a bit after one. We decided to go in my car because I didn't want to drive the city-owned one. Hump and I split the driving time while Art leaned back, stretched out his legs, and tried to get three more hours of sleep. I didn't wake him until we reached the city limits of Fletcherville.

It's a farm town, like a hundred others across the state. There's a main street about a block long. A J.C. Penney store, a few small shops, a movie theater showing a double feature of horror films, the Wagonwheel Cafe, and a hotel, The Planter's Rest.

Hump pulled to the curb, and I got the attention of a kid wearing jeans and a Braves t-shirt. "Where's the police department?"

"Take the next left," he said. "It's just past Law Court."

Hump worked over into the lane and made the turn. It was a narrow street, still paved with the old red bricks. In places, the bricks were worn down into ruts, and it was slow driving. It wasn't comfortable, but I guess I understood why some historical society or other probably opposed paving over the bricks. The street most likely went back to the days when the only vehicles in the town were wagons.

Low two-story buildings of the same brick edged in from both sides of the street. I assumed this was Law Court, because of all the lawyers' signs sticking out of the building fronts at all levels. I counted about thirty shingles. I shook my head. I couldn't see that many lawyers making a living in a town that small.

And then we were past Law Court and back in the real world. The police station building looked new, built in the last five or six years, I guessed. The sign out front had Fletcherville Police Department on it, and below that, in small script, Jail in Back. Hump pulled into a gravel parking lot on the other side of the building. He parked next to a police cruiser and a pickup truck.

Art got out and spent a minute trying to shake the wrinkles out of his jacket. "Coming in?" he asked.

I nodded.

"I've been in enough police stations," Hump said.

We left him stretching and lighting a cigarette. We went in. A chest-high counter stretched across the front of the room. There wasn't anyone at the counter. A young man with his legs propped up on the typewriter leaf of a desk looked at us, but didn't get to his feet. He was wearing a dark cotton police uniform.

"Do something for you?" he asked.

"Where's the chief?" Art asked.

"He's out," the young cop said.

"I'd like to see him."

"You can take a seat or come back in an hour."

"I don't plan on waiting an hour," Art said, an edge in his voice. "How about you calling him?"

"I know his answer now," the young cop said. "He'll say he'll be back in an hour."

"Come over here. I'm tired of yelling."

The policeman dropped his legs from the typewriter leaf and got up slowly. He came toward us like he was prepared for almost any kind of trouble we planned on making. When he reached the counter, Art got out his I.D. case and opened it.

"I just drove all the way from Atlanta, and I'm not even on shift time, and I don't have any intention of cooling my heels for an hour. How about you calling the chief, and telling him it's police business?"

The chief threw the front door open ten minutes later. He was red-faced and angry. "What's all this Goddamned rush?"

The young policeman nodded in the direction of Art.

The chief was spare and lean. His hands and face had the washed-out wintertime look of a man who fished all summer. He leaned on the counter and looked at Art. Art passed him the ID case. While the chief looked at it, Art told him about Crystal Hanner and the fact that she was needed for questioning in the killings that had taken place in Atlanta in the last few days.

"The two whores?" the chief said. "I read about that."

"The Hanner girl knew one of them and might be able to tell us something."

"You got any idea how you're going to find her?" The chief closed the ID case and passed it back to Art.

"She got in pretty late last night. Might be in the hotel."

"What's that name again?" The chief pulled a telephone toward him and dialed a number.

"Crystal Hanner."

"Bob, this is the chief. You got a girl named Crystal Hanner registered over there?" He turned to us. "He's checking the cards." After a minute, he said, "Yes, Bob? Is that right?" He shook his head at Art. "Nobody by that name over there."

"See if any woman checked in last night ... no matter what the name is."

The chief mumbled into the phone.

"A blonde with dark roots showing? Mid-twenties, kind of tall?"

The chief read that into the phone. He paused and then asked, "You there, Bob, when she checked in?"

"It would have been after midnight," Art said.

"She's there," the chief said. "Registered as Mrs. Carol Howard."

"I'd like to pick her up," Art said.

"You want to question her here?"

"I need her back in Atlanta."

The chief turned to the young cop. "Go with them, Ernie."

"Right, Chief."

Art thanked the chief and told him, if he was ever in Atlanta, to stop by. The chief said he would, and it might be soon. He leaned on the counter and gave a long sigh as he watched us leave. His day had been ruined, but he could console himself with the thought that he'd done some police business.

I stood outside room 28 and knocked.

"Who is it?" It was a woman's voice.

"Room service," I said.

"I didn't order anything."

"Room service," I said, with the same level of voice, as if I hadn't heard her.

The door opened, and I put a hand on it and pushed. At first, just seeing me and not knowing me, I thought she was going to faint. Then Art stepped from behind me and she recognized him. It was relief mixed with anger.

"Back to Atlanta," Art said.

Hump drove. Art was in the back seat with Crystal, and I was up front, turning with an arm on the seat back to listen to Art's questioning and add my dime's worth now and then.

"That wasn't smart, Crystal," Art said.

"I didn't have any choice."

"Why not?"

"I could have got in trouble if I'd stayed in Atlanta," she said.

"You are in trouble," Art said. "You set us up."

"Who'd you call from the Central Hotel after Art dropped you off?" I asked.

"I didn't call anybody."

"You called somebody, or those four goons wouldn't have known where to find us."

"I didn't make any call," she insisted.

"Just give me a name," I said.

Hump said, "Let me pull over to the side of the road. After she set me up last night, I wouldn't mind beating the crap out of her."

"This is Hump," I said. "He doesn't like being set up. He likes to believe he can trust people."

"Believe me," she said to Hump.

"Who'd you call?" Art pushed at her.

"A name and a phone number," I said.

"Otherwise, it's going to be a long afternoon and night," Hump said.

"I can't tell you what I don't know."

"Who'd you call from the lobby?" Art nodded at me, and I passed him my pack of smokes. He lit one and blew the smoke at her.

"I didn't make a call."

"The desk clerk says you did."

"He's lying, then."

"You're the one lying," Hump said. There was a turn-off coming up on our right. Hump went into the turn going pretty fast. It threw us all to the side. I banged a shoulder against the door. It was a clay dirt road, not paved. Hump braked in a whirl of red dust, and was out of the car in a rush. He pulled the rear door open and yanked the girl out by an arm. His right hand went back, like he was about to slap the hell out of her. "Bitch! I'm tired of your lying."

"No," Crystal shouted at him. "I called this guy I know. I told him I had to leave town, and why."

"His name?" Hump still had the hand back.

"Alan Wright. His name is Alan Wright."

"See how easy it is?" Hump pushed her back into the car and closed the door, and got behind the wheel again. He got turned around and we headed for Atlanta once more.

"A pimp?" Art asked.

"Yes."

"Yours?"

I got out my pack and offered her a smoke. She took one and Art lit it for her.

"Mine," she said.

"He the type to send four guys, muscle men, after us?"

"Alan? He wouldn't have the guts. All he knows is how…"

"You think he called somebody else?"

"He might have." She spread her hands and looked at Art. "I wasn't there. I have no way of knowing if he called anybody after I called him."

No way to argue with that. Art got out his pad and took down Alan Wright's address. It was an apartment on Piedmont, on the west side of the park. It was, Crystal said with a misguided pride, near the Piedmont Driving Club, the most exclusive of the Atlanta social clubs.

"Am I going back to jail?"

"For the time being," Art said. "Until we've leaned on Alan Wright and checked your story out."

"I wish I didn't have to."

That floated in the silence for a time. Now that we had out of her what we wanted, there didn't seem to be much to say. I watched her and saw that she'd accepted the prospect of jail. She relaxed and, when I saw that, I could ask my questions.

"How well did you know Joy Lynn Barrow?"

"I never knew her," Crystal said.

"Look, are we going to have to go through this every time?"

"What?"

"This lying. You lived in the same apartment on St. Charles, and you had the same pimp, Harry Falk."

"All right, so I knew her for a few weeks. I didn't like her, and she kept making trouble between Harry and me."

"How?"

"She thought she was his bottom woman and his only woman. Jealous? God, the way she acted! Like he belonged to her. And she was such a poor hustler. I could make more with one hand in a night that she could with her whole ass."

"How long did you share the apartment?"

"Not long. I couldn't trick, with all that shit going on."

"What happened?"

"Harry set me up in my own place," she said.

PIMP FOR THE DEAD

"That easy?"

"I was the best money-maker he had."

"How many girls did Harry have in his stable at the time?"

"The two of us, at first. Later there was another girl, but she was out of a freak show."

"The dwarf girl, Carol?"

"That's the one," she said. "God, who would want to ball her?"

"Harry, I guess."

"That was like him. You know why I left him?"

I shook my head.

"He went down to Miami for a few days. Came back with the clap and gave it to all three of us. Right then, I knew I'd had enough. You might slip up now and then and get a dose from a john, but from your own best man? That's something a girl doesn't have to live with."

"When was that?"

"In the fall sometime. Late September or October."

"You see Joy Lynn after that?"

She shrugged. "Now and then, here and there. She hated me. You know the kind of crazy head she had on her? She thought I gave Harry that dose of clap. After I left, I guess that was what he told her."

"You heard what happened to Harry?"

"That's no loss," she said. "Big cock, small brain."

"That's quite an epitaph," Art said.

"Now you take Alan. He's different." She'd started glowing, and then she stopped and turned it off. She'd just remembered that she'd sold Alan out to us. "Too bad about him. He had style."

"What'll you do now?" I asked.

"Stay out of it, for a while."

Art was watching her face. "It's getting rough out on the street, huh?"

"I don't know anything about that," she said.

"It must be," Art said, "if you're going to drop out."

"I'm getting religion." She fluttered her eyelids at Art and then at me. It was a Lillian Gish parody. "It's been coming on me for a long time."

We went by my place and Art put Crystal in his unmarked car. We tail-gated him downtown to the station, where he dropped off Crystal. I didn't know what the charge was going to be. I knew, at the same time, he could come up with one. It wasn't hard to find a reason to jug a hooker with a past record like Crystal's.

When she got out of the car, she turned to Hump and me, smiled, and blew us a kiss. As the hand waved the kiss toward us, it changed. It became the high middle finger: *up yours.*

# CHAPTER SEVEN

The security man at the door didn't want to let us in without calling up to Alan Wright's apartment first. Art pressed him a bit. He called him a number of names, and he ended up threatening to call for a half-dozen cruisers, sirens going, so it would look like we were knocking over a three-dollar whorehouse. Either that, or we'd go in and make the arrest in a quiet way.

"Well, if it's going to be an arrest," the security man said lamely, "I wouldn't try to stand in your way."

"Now you're being sweet," Art said.

I stopped Art before we reached the bank of elevators. "You believe him?"

"Huh?"

"Why don't you keep him company for a few minutes?"

"Why...?"

"He might call up and warn Wright," I said.

Art pivoted and looked at the security man. "You think that's necessary, huh?" But he was working it around in his head. He didn't mind it at all. He was limited in what he could do, limited by the rights and the court, but Hump and I weren't. We knew gutter talk.

"How long?"

"Ten minutes," I said.

Art checked his watch and walked back across the lobby to stand beside the security guard. He started talking to the guard and, just before Hump and I stepped into the elevator, he called over to us, "He's got a girl with him."

On the ride up to the 7th floor Hump asked, "You got any ideas?"

"About getting in? How about some lying?"

"I could tell him I'm the new security guard..."

"Yeah?"

"And somebody just broke the windshield of his car with a brick."

I grinned at him. "You think he'll believe a cock-and-bull story like that?"

"Let's find out."

"Oh, shit, yes."

"You say what?"

The door edged open a bit more. I could see the big dark-haired stud in the blue silk robe and slippers. His hair was pillow-mussed, and he put up a hand and tried to smooth it down.

"My car? A white Mercedes sedan?"

"That's the one, sir," Hump said. "I could see the brick, right there on the front seat."

"You called the police yet?"

"I wanted to make sure it was yours first." He reached in his pocket and brought out a scrap of paper. "Look, I wrote down the license number, and if you'll check it..."

Wright nodded and reached out a hand for whatever Hump had in his hand. Hump caught the wrist and yanked him forward. Wright slammed against the doorframe. Wright pulled against him. "Hey, what the hell...?" Hump let the wrist go and Wright went off balance, falling back into the room. Hump pushed the door open and went after him. It was with the same quickness and the speed I'd seen him use on those fall afternoons when he'd gone after a quarterback or a back taking a swing pass in his area.

I walked in after him and closed the door.

Wright had more balls than Crystal Hanner said he did. He came up and moved toward Hump, you could say that for him. He didn't let Hump's size bother him. He flicked a left and Hump ignored it. Then he threw a right that Hump took on his forearm. At the same time, Hump flipped the right upwards and stepped under it. He hit Wright about belly-high, and Wright grunted and farted and sat down on the plush carpet. The fight was over.

Hump turned on me. "You just going to stand there?"

I grinned at him and left him massaging the forearm where Wright had hit him. I crossed the living room, filling my eyes with all the expensive crap you could doll an apartment up with if you could talk a few women into selling their asses for you. The door to the bedroom was closed. That was polite of Wright, protecting the reputation of the woman. Before he set her out on the street. I turned the knob and went in. The lighting was low in the bedroom.

The naked girl had her back to me. High-rumped and well-formed, her hair was honey-colored and shoulder-length. I might have stood there and admired her some more, except for the fact that she was dialing a number on the phone. I crossed the thick-carpeted bedroom in a lope and caught her around the waist with one hand. I used the other hand to jerk the receiver away from her and jam it back on its cradle. Then I could use both hands on her, and I needed them. She struggled and twisted, and once or twice I got a handful of titty without being able to enjoy it. She swung an elbow at me and kicked back. But there is a kind of disadvantage about being naked. It makes a person feel defenseless, and nothing you try then ever seems to work.

I swung her around and threw her onto the bed. She faced me then. A little girl's face attached to a body that had just reached it, the plateau, the full ripeness that has a few good years left before the skin tone's shot.

"I'm not going to hurt you." I reached down to the baseboard and pulled out the phone jack. "You got a robe?" I waved the phone at the closet. "How about in there?"

She shook her head.

Eyes still on her, I backed into a walk-in closet. Over in the back corner there was about a yard of shirts on hangers. I yanked out the first one I reached and carried it into the bedroom. I tossed it to her. "Put this on."

"Who are you?" Her hands fumbled with the shirt, trying to get the top button undone so she could remove the hanger.

"Don't worry yourself about it."

She got into the shirt and buttoned it all the way down the front. It reached her knees. When she rolled up the sleeves they wadded at her wrists.

I nodded toward the living room door. "After you."

Hump must have lifted Alan Wright and put him into one of the rope-bottomed chairs while I was in the bedroom. Wright was bent over, hands clasping his stomach, gasping for breath. "I think you broke something."

"Nothing in there to break that I know of," Hump said. He eased around slowly and looked the girl up and down. "Well, what do we have here?"

"Some meatroll Wright's getting ready to turn out," I said.

"We're engaged," the girl said.

"Sure." I winked at Hump, making it broad enough for her to see. "He's engaged to his whole stable." I waved her to the sofa. I tossed the phone into an empty chair.

The girl sat down and stuffed the shirttail between her thighs. Hump watched this and grinned at me. "You get all the good jobs. Why do I always get left in the living room?"

"It's the class system." I dipped my head at Wright. "You talk to our boy yet?"

"Right now, I'm waiting to see if he's going to keep his supper down."

"It's his rug," I said, "so it doesn't matter."

"True enough."

"We're going to play a game called truth or lies. Everybody knows how to play it, except we've got some new rules. Every time he lies, I want you to cuff him in the mouth, the nose or the ears."

"Who are you?" Wright demanded. "You know, you could be in a lot of trouble."

"We just got back from Fletcherville, and we brought back another girl you're engaged to."

"I don't know anybody from Fletcherville."

I looked at Hump. "You believe that?"

Hump answered me by reaching out and cuffing Wright across the mouth. The swing looked effortless, like there wasn't any steam behind it, but it had the flattened-out shock of a pistol shot.

Hump said, "Crystal Hanner said to say hello."

"Oh, her?" Wright lifted a hand and rubbed it across his mouth. "Sure, I know her."

"She said she called you last night. She told you she was in a bind with a cop, and she was supposed to ..."

"I haven't seen her in weeks. The last time I saw her ..."

Hump leaned in and backhanded him across the nose. "I don't think he understands the game yet."

"It'll slip up on him." I pushed it back at Wright. "Not long after that call to you, four hard-asses keep the appointment instead of Crystal. My question is, did you send them?"

"I don't know any four ..."

Hump popped him in the left ear. "I don't think this game is much fun," he said to me, "when the other people playing it cheat."

"Either you sent them yourself, or you know who did send them," I said.

"I don't know ..."

Hump cuffed him in the mouth again. A thin trickle of blood curled over the corner of Wright's mouth and ran down his chin. His tongue flicked out and touched it and tasted the salt.

"You send them?"

Wright shook his head.

"See?" I said to Hump. "He's learning to play the game." I got out a smoke and lit it. "So you called somebody. Who'd you call?"

"I didn't…"

Leaning in, Hump popped him across the nose.

"Who'd you call?"

"I told you, I didn't…"

Hump hit him in the nose again. A glob of blood and snot poured out of his left nostril. He sniffed at it but he couldn't stop it. He reached up and smeared it with the palm of his hand. "Does she have to stay here?"

"No reason." I curled a finger at the girl. "You. Come here." I followed her into the bedroom. "Flop. Make yourself comfortable." Then, shielded from the living room, I put my back to her and got out one of the hundreds I'd gotten from Barrow. Using a felt-tip pen, I wrote J.H. in the top left corner of the bill. I folded the bill and hid it in my palm.

In the living room, Wright was worrying the blood around his mouth and nose. He'd smeared it into a thin coat over the lower half of his face. I took one look at him and went back into the bedroom. There was a box of Kleenex on the table next to the bed. I pulled out a thick wad. At that sound, the girl opened her eyes and looked at him. "You're going to kill him, aren't you?"

"If we have to," I said.

Her eyes jerked shut and a tear ran out of her right eye. Oh, shit. Whore or no whore, it was a nasty business. Without looking back at her, I went into the living room. I handed the wad of Kleenex to Wright. Hump gave me a puzzled look. He didn't know what was going on. "I think you're messing up your robe." Leaning toward him, I pulled at the robe. The other hand, the one with the hundred in it, edged toward the robe pocket. The hundred dropped into his pocket without a rustle.

The doorbell rang. I went over and opened it for Art. Art looked at Alan Wright and then at us. "What's going on here?"

"Chief, we've got him. Pimping, pandering, whatever you want to call it." I pointed at the bedroom door. "The girl's in there."

Art crossed the room and looked in the bedroom. "That's a girl, sure enough."

"He offered us the girl, the two of us for a hundred."

"That's a goddam lie," Wright shouted. "You two came busting in here, and ..."

"The marked bill's in his robe pocket. I saw him put it there."

"That's right.". Hump understood the charade and grinned at me.

Wright reared up out of the chair. Hump reached out a big arm and wrapped it around his neck. Art reached into the robe pocket and brought out the hundred.

"My mark's on it," I said.

Art unfolded the bill slowly. "That's your mark, all right." He turned to Wright. "You ever do time?"

"It's a frame. A goddam frame, and you know it."

"We'll leave that to the judge." Art walked over to the bedroom door. "Get your clothes on, girl."

"I'd better watch her," Hump said. "She might try to hide some drugs on her, or something."

"Why not?" Art said.

"It won't hold up," Wright said. "I'll be out in twenty-four hours."

"Twenty-four hours might be enough." Art watched Hump go into the bedroom. "Keep your hands off her."

"I don't see why. I paid for the whole hog." Hump went in and closed the door behind him.

Wright watched the door close and licked at his lips. "I am engaged to Elaine."

"Sure," I said, "the two-week engagement, before you buy her some walking shoes."

From beyond the bedroom door, there was a choked scream and Hump's deep laughter. The scream bothered Art and he turned to me. I shook my head. I knew Hump better than that, but Wright didn't.

"Look, are you going to let that black ape…?"

"It won't wear out," I said.

Another choked scream. Wright flinched. "That girl is my…"

"You shouldn't chippy with your own girls," I said.

"All right." The sand and grit poured out of him and made an invisible pile at his feet. "I called Ed Buddy after Crystal called me."

"Who's he?"

"Out of town. Chicago, I think."

"He the one doing the organizing?"

Wright nodded. "I already paid my dues."

"How much?"

He turned and looked at the closed bedroom door. It was quiet in there. "A hundred a week for each girl in the stable."

"That's high," I said.

"It's better than having to bury them."

"Or getting buried."

"That too," he said.

"What's the phone number?"

He rattled it off from memory. Art had him repeat it, so he could write it down.

"How do we reach him?"

"That's all I know. The phone number."

I stepped away from them and threw the bedroom door open. "She dressed?"

Hump pushed her into the living room. She was fully dressed and, if she'd been a cat, she'd have been hissing.

"Didn't mind dressing," Hump said. "But she's not much of a screamer."

"How?" I asked.

"Pinched her ass blue."

Art went into the bedroom with Wright while he got dressed. He gave the bedroom a frisk. In the night table next to the bed he found a gold coke spoon and a film can with a couple of table-spoons of cocaine in it. He called me into the bedroom. "Now it's a drug bust."

"Then you won't need the other evidence." I held out my hand.

He stared at me blankly. "Huh?"

"The hundred."

He shook his head and passed it back to me.

The paddy wagon came a few minutes later. He was trying out some ideas on me, wanting some way he could make the charges without admitting that he'd violated Wright's rights. I think he finally decided that the pandering thing had led to the search that uncovered the cocaine. It might get by, and then again it might not.

"When did they move out?" I asked.

The night security guard, an old man who walked with the pain of bad joints, led the three of us down the hall to suite 17, in the old building on Mitchell. It was an office building for companies on the way up or the way down.

"They didn't exactly move out," the old man said. "Not offi-cially, anyway." He unlocked the door to suite 17 and went in. He fumbled to the right of the door and switched on the overhead lights. "They went out for a coffee break this morning and didn't come back."

The main piece of furniture in the room was a long table with about twenty telephones on it, each phone bracketed on the sides by soundproof partitions. At one end of the table there was a huge stack of Atlanta phone book pages. I stepped past the old man and picked up one of the phones. The line was dead. "What was it?"

"What they call a boiler room."

I looked at Art.

"Used for telephone selling. Sell you anything from a carpet to a magazine."

There was a closed door to the right and an open one straight ahead. Art and Hump, followed by the old man, went to the open door. I rounded the table and pushed the other door open. It was a bathroom, with a fetid scent locked in there. A toilet, a roll of paper, some paper towels and a thin wedge of soap. And a single turd floating in the toilet bowl.

The other room in the suite was the office. A battered old desk filled most of the room. There was a swivel chair behind it and a metal cabinet in the rear left corner. The file drawers were pulled out, sagging. Art turned from the file cabinet and shook his head. "Empty."

The desk was clean, too. From behind the desk, Hump nudged the metal trash can with his toe and I went over and looked into it. Nothing but some cigarette ashes. I turned back to the desk and, being careful not to touch the phone grip, I lifted the receiver by the ends and heard the dial tone.

"This is the working phone."

At the doorway, Art was talking to the security guard.

"...said they were going to do a telephone survey," the old man said.

"They say what kind?"

"Not that I heard."

"They take a long lease?" Art asked.

"The regular year one," he said. He shook his head and looked around. "A lot of good that lease'll do anybody. I came on tonight and found the place cleaned out, like it is. You don't work a place like this without getting some hunches. I called the day man. He said they'd been in early and left, and didn't come back. Downstairs, I got this list of home phone numbers for the lease holders. We keep them in case of an emergency."

"And you called the number?"

"It was a church ... the Baptist one near 5th and Peachtree."

"That's a new one on me," Hump said, "giving a church number."

We were out on the sidewalk in front of the building. The old man was seated in a folding chair reading the evening paper. Now and then he'd lower the paper and look out the doorway at us.

"Maybe they planned it that way, maybe they didn't."

"And if they had had to call the number? Say some time last week?"

"Easy enough," I said. "A smart hustler just asks to see the list, and he says something about no wonder they didn't reach him. This digit or that digit is wrong, and he corrects it."

"And the number is good until the next time," Art said.

"And we're no closer to Ed Buddy, if that's his real name." I got out my smokes and offered them around.

"You could expect it," Art said. "The four studs didn't report back last night when they were supposed to. That meant something had gone sour. They really cleared out last night, probably just dropped by today to give it a fast once-over, to make sure it was clean."

"It worked for them for the wrong reason," I said. "Those four last night ... they call anybody from the jail?"

Art shook his head. "That was probably built into the deal. No calls. No strings that go back to the men who hired them. So they must have made their own bail."

"They're out?"

"Yes."

I looked up at the old building. "And we're dead-ended."

I drove Hump over to my place to get his car. Then I left him and wheeled across town to Marcy's apartment. It's in one of those sprawling apartment complexes. Since she moved in, this will be the first spring there'll be grass to cover the red clay that used to blow all over the place. Maybe this spring the water in the swimming pool won't look like orange soda pop.

I found Marcy back in the kitchen, seated at the table with the diary propped open in front of her, a can of tuna and a can of beef stew at the top corners.

"How's it going?" I blew in her ear, and then went over to the refrigerator and got a can of beer.

"It's ruining my life. I do some decoding before I leave for work, during my breaks and during lunch, and I start again as soon as I get back home in the evening."

"Any progress?"

She pushed a sheaf of pages toward me. I sipped my beer and read through the entries. Marcy must have gotten into the spirit of the thing. The translation seemed to go a lot faster now. I guess it became drill after a time: moving the final letter up to the front of the word, and not having to think which numeral stood for which vowel.

In the pages she'd decoded since the night before, Crystal Hanner's story checked out. Joy Lynn almost crowed when Crystal moved out. She saw it as a victory for herself in her relationship with Harry. And a few days later she welcomed the arrival of Carol, the dwarf girl. She didn't see Carol as a threat, and she found herself really liking the doll-like girl. It was better working the streets with her. Carol didn't count tricks on her, and she didn't keep tabs on Carol, either. Now the stash money jumped back up to between $60 and $90 a night, and continued to grow. In one entry Harry bitched about the income falling, and she made herself a promise to use some of the put-by money on nights when the tricks didn't come, or when the weather was bad.

I pushed the pages back across the table to Marcy. "Work's going damn good," I said.

She mimicked it back to me. "Why don't you do some of it?"

"I will. Where's the address book?"

"That'll be a big help," Marcy said. "It'll save me about twenty minutes, if that."

"If you don't want me to ...?"

She passed the address book to me. I got a clean sheet of paper and began. It was slow going for me. I had to write the vowels and the numbers that represented them on the top of the page. Each time I got to a numeral, I had to stop and look at my key. Even with that trouble, I got through most of them in a bit more than half an hour. I was on the next to the last one on the list, when it hit me.

D2 5DDYB

I got up and walked around the table. I put the address book in front of Marcy, a thumb under the two words. "Is this what I think?"

"Ed Buddy," she said.

"The rest of it?"

She read it off with hardly a pause. "New in town. Address when settled."

I straightened up. "The problem just changed." I returned to my seat and wrote it out in big letters on a sheet of paper: D2 5DDYB. "From now on I want you to skim the entries and decode only those that have to do with an Ed or an Ed Buddy."

"Why?"

"Just do it." Then I softened it "This is the first real break. The diary might give us a hunch, a way of reaching this Buddy guy."

"So far, she's never named any of the johns," Marcy said.

"That might be before she started her list."

"All right." She didn't sound convinced. "I'm stopping for the night now. I'll start again in the morning."

"I'd rather you didn't."

"Huh?"

"This is important, Marcy. I want you to go on, even if you have to call in sick in the morning."

"Slave driver."

"Sorry." I walked around the table and kissed her. "I hate to ask it of you."

"You going to stay with me?"

"I'd be a distraction," I said.

"So you're going to bed, and I'm going to stay up all night?"

"I hope it doesn't take that long." I eased toward the door.

"On the shelf over there."

"What?"

"The seeds you wanted," she said.

It was a bundle of seed packages with a rubber band holding them together. I scooped them off the shelf and left, before she had time to come after me swinging, or started throwing things.

At home, I sat down in my kitchen and drank a nightcap. While drinking, I slipped the rubber band and fanned out the seed packages. Corn, summer squash, zucchini, speckled butter beans and Chinese cabbage. Chinese cabbage? I flipped the package and looked at the picture on the front. It didn't look like any vegetable I'd ever eaten. I thought about calling Marcy and asking her what the hell we wanted with Chinese cabbage, but I fought the urge. I didn't want to bother her until she'd finished her surface skimming of the diary.

And maybe, just maybe, the Chinese cabbage was her idea of a joke.

I thought I'd been asleep only about ten minutes. The clock on the night table put it at three hours. I was gunning up to be pissed, when I realized that it was probably Marcy. I answered the phone on about the fifth ring.

It wasn't Marcy. It was Hump. I didn't recognize his voice at first. It was distorted by hard breathing and an edge of pain.

"Hardman...?"

"What's wrong? You sound..."

"Just listen. Four studs just left my place. Did some working me over. Might be coming to your place next."

"Who?"

"I think it was the same four from that bar."

"How are you?"

"I've got some lumps, and I think a broken wrist."

"I'll be there soon as I can," I said.

"Watch yourself."

As soon as the line went dead, I made a run for the closet. I got down the cigar box from the top shelf, from behind a number of other boxes. It was where I kept my cash and my .38 Police Positive. I put the box back and kept the .38. I dressed quickly. Slacks, sport shirt and loafers without socks. I struggled into a jacket and stuck the .38 in my waistband.

I went out the back door, low and bent over and eyes sweeping the yard, knowing every shape there and looking for the one that didn't belong. The shapes and shadows appeared to fit, and I moved around the corner of the house toward the garage. I stopped there and stared down the driveway out to the street. The mama cat came out of the darkness and rubbed against my leg. I used a foot to push her away as gently as I could.

Nothing. Nothing moved. It was twenty minutes or so by car from Hump's apartment to mine, and if Hump had called me right away there was no way they could have reached my place yet. And every minute I wasted being careful and foxy put them closer. If they were coming at all.

I sucked it up and walked over to my car. I stood by the hood and remained still, reading the yard and the road and the hedge on the far side of the yard. Nothing. I got into the car, kicked over the engine and backed out.

I made it to Hump's apartment in fifteen minutes. That included three or four red lights I ran on the way. And one red light I had to wait out when a police cruiser began to tail me.

# CHAPTER EIGHT

rt Maloney arrived about the time the ambulance did. Hump hadn't wanted the ambulance, but I insisted. Besides the broken left wrist, he'd taken some bad licks about the head. One eye, his right one, was swollen closed, and there was a cut in his lip and, past that, when he talked, I could see a chipped tooth.

"How'd it happen?"

I stepped in and told it for Hump. It saved Hump some breath and some energy. Hump had been out having a few drinks. He got back to his apartment a bit after two a.m. He hadn't been expecting trouble, and he'd been boxed easily. He'd been about halfway up the outside stairs when the first two stepped out of the darkness of the landing. He was trying to move back and set himself, when the other two—he hadn't heard them approaching from behind—came up from the street and boxed him in. His first awareness of those two was a hard shot he took in the back. The two from the dark doorway moved in then. His left wrist got broken early. He'd seen the club coming down, and he put up an arm to ward it off. That put him at a disadvantage, and he'd taken a lot of punishment until he used a shoulder and his good arm to wrest a club away from one of the attackers. When he started swinging the club around, they'd left in a hurry.

"What kind of club?" Art asked.

I walked over to the telephone table. I picked up the club and brought it back to Art. It was about three feet long, one end rounded and the other sawed off unevenly. I slapped it in the palm of my hand.

"Oak, I think."

Art took it. He nodded. "From a hoe or a rake handle."

The ambulance attendants were ready to go. They'd considered bringing up a stretcher, but Hump hadn't wanted that, and the attendants took a long look at Hump's 270 pounds and went along with him. It wouldn't have been much of a pleasure, carting that weight down a couple of flights of stairs.

I went out into the hallway with Hump. "I'll be over in a few minutes," I said. "Art and I want to check something out."

"See you then," he said and went down the stairs, partly supported by the attendants.

Art was on the phone when I got back to the apartment. "Let it go, then. We'll have to try it from another angle." He hung up and shook his head. "That was the cruiser I sent over to check the address the four gave when they put up bail."

"No luck?"

"A deserted house on King's Court Road."

"So they jumped bail."

"It looks that way."

I looked around the apartment. I picked up the club and cut out the lights. I locked the door and we went down the stairs. Art nodded at the club.

"What's that for?"

"Hump might want to return it to the owner, if he gets a chance."

I waited out in the hall at Grady while they set Hump's wrist and cleaned up his cuts and bruises. At one point, an intern came out of the emergency room and lit a cigarette. He leaned on the desk and smiled at the nurse. He said, in a voice with a touch of Mississippi or Alabama in it, "That jig in there must have a head that's solid bone." The nurse shook her head and frowned, nodding in my direction, as if to shut him up.

"Oh." He pranced over to me. "You with Mr. Evans?"

I said I was.

"I think he ought to stay here a day or two, for observation. He won't hear of it. I think he's making a mistake."

"It's his own mistake," I said.

"He'll have to sign a release."

"Take it to him then," I said.

After he left, I went over to the nurse and told her where she could bill me. She seemed reluctant, so I got out a wad of cash and paid the charges. The fact of payment turned her sweet again, and she smiled at me several times while I leaned up against the wall and waited.

Hump came out looking shaky. They'd put a short cast on his left wrist. They'd also shaved his hair in several places, and I could see the bristle of some stitches.

I took his arm. "You sure you don't want to stay overnight?"

"I'm sure."

A police cruiser was pulled up in front of my house. A uniformed cop with a riot gun met us when we got out of my car in the driveway. He wasn't pointing the riot gun, but it was at the ready.

"You Mr. Hardman?"

I said I was.

"Maloney said for us to wait for you, and then check the house and yard."

"Glad to have you," I said.

One policeman checked the house with me while the other one searched the backyard. There wasn't any sign that anyone had been in the house after I'd left for Hump's apartment. Before they left, they said a cruiser would be checking by every hour on the hour. I thanked them and saw them leave.

Over Hump's protest, I gave him the bed and made up the sofa for me. It was after four when I got into bed. It took me a long time to drop off. There was too much working around in my head, and I had to take the time to empty it out.

❧ ❧ ❧

Hump was in the kitchen having a cup of coffee when I woke up. I padded in barefooted and looked him over.

"How you feel?"

"Like a bad Sunday morning."

"Dizziness? Sick at your stomach?"

He shook his head. "Like a toothache in my wrist."

"You might live," I said, "but you're not going to be pretty for a month or so."

"Who wants to be pretty all year 'round?"

Breakfast just about cleaned out my refrigerator. I was putting the breakfast dishes in to soak when Art called.

"Odd thing," Art said. "I told you those four didn't make a call the other night after the brawl at the Book Store ... when they were taken to the station and booked. That's true enough. But it turns out that a lawyer showed up later, without being called, and helped set up the bail."

"Who was the lawyer?"

"Denton Hughes," Art said.

"That one." I didn't know Hughes. I'd heard of him. He had the reputation of being a racket lawyer. He seemed to specialize in defending night club owners against state and city attempts to revoke their liquor licenses. In most of these cases, the state and city contention was that criminal money was involved in the ownership, and that the license holders were merely front men. Of course, none of that proved he was a racket lawyer. As long as a defendant had a right to a trial, he had a right to a lawyer. But it was getting clearer and clearer that he was being touched by the pitch.

"What are you going to do?" Art asked.

"I might go visit him."

"No rough stuff."

"Of course not," I said.

I shaved and showered and dressed in my best spring suit, a light tan one that I'd sent out for cleaning when I'd seen the spring coming. Near the end, I went into the kitchen and got the black shoe polish and the shine rag from the clutter drawer. Hump watched me put on a slapdash shine.

"You got fancy business this morning?"

"Going to see the lawyer who was representing the four muscle men."

"I'll go with you," Hump said.

"You up to it?"

He nodded.

"You'll scare the hell out of him."

"Isn't that what it's all about?"

I had another cup of coffee while Hump dressed. When he was ready, I drove downtown to the First Federal Building. We parked in the lot across the street and rode the elevator up to the tenth floor, to the office of Denton Hughes and Associates.

The secretary in the outer office, pigeon proud and haughty, started the snot right away. "If you don't have an appointment with Mr. Hughes, it will be impossible for him to see you. Mr. Hughes is a very busy man."

"Tell him it's about the four men he represented in the fight at the Book Store." I clutched the rolled-up paper bag under one arm.

"I'm certain he won't ..."

"Try him," I said.

It was a money office. If you didn't know already, you knew when you saw the office. It said things like, *it costs money to hire this man,* or *a hundred dollars won't buy you much here.* Decorator-done, with all the stops pulled. Dark panel walls that looked like they might have come out of a mansion in this country or a castle somewhere else. Moody hunting prints kept the somber tone. A small alcove faced the secretary's desk. There were four black leather chairs near a low table. On the low table, not the usual waiting room magazines, but a scattering of Christmas coffee-table books, the ones created for gift-giving at twenty-five or fifty dollars.

The secretary didn't use the intercom. She got up and showed us the kind of hips I call armchair-stuffed and the legs and ass of a ballet dancer. She opened the door to the inner office only wide enough to slip through sideways.

She was back in two or three minutes. She eased the door closed behind her and said, "Mr. Hughes does not understand why you wish to see him, but if you wish to make an appointment he may be able to see you in a few days."

"Is that right?" I took the paper bag from under my arm and began unrolling it. "When do you think he might have time for me?"

"I would have to check his calendar, but I think we might find fifteen minutes for you in a week or ten days."

I opened the bag and reached down into it. "Is that the best you can do?"

"Of course, it may be later," she said.

"I can't wait that long." I wrapped my fingers around the three-foot length of hoe or rake handle and dropped the bag. "I think now will be just fine with me."

Her eyes took in the length of oak handle. She put up an arm to bar the door, but Hump reached out a long arm and caught her by the back of the neck. He jerked her out of the doorway. I hit the door with an elbow and walked in.

Denton Hughes looked up from behind about two thousand dollars worth of desk. Dark hair peppered with gray, a full but neat mustache, and a suntan from a health club or spa. A lean five-ten, and about fifty years of age. All that money could buy and had bought.

He hesitated for the count of about five. He blinked a couple of times, and then he leaned forward and reached for the telephone on the front corner of his desk. I moved in fast and swung the piece of oak handle. The phone shattered at the grip. I missed his hand by an inch or two.

"I think we ought to talk today," I said.

Hump stepped into the office, pushing the girl in front of him.

"The gentleman with me is Hump Evans." I held out the oak club. "This was used on him last night by four of your clients. He's got a broken wrist and some other lumps. We'd like to talk to your four clients."

He did it easy, leaning back in his chair and drawing back the hand that he'd frozen near the phone. "That should be easy enough." He lifted a large address book from the corner of his desk and placed it directly in front of him. "I assume you're talking about the gentlemen who were in the brawl at the Book Store Bar?"

I nodded.

He flipped the book open and his finger traced its way over a page or so of listings. He looked up at me. "The address is 2112 King's Court Road."

I shook my head. "That's not good enough. It's a deserted house."

"Is that so?" He shook his head slowly. "That's odd."

"I think so too." I reached out and tapped the front edge of the desk with the oak handle. It didn't chip, but I think it dented. "Try again for us."

"It's as much a mystery to me as it is to you," he said.

"It doesn't bother you that they've jumped their bond?"

"Not really. The bondsman is the one who took the risk."

"Just as long as you got your fee ahead of time."

He nodded.

"They don't sound like your kind of client," I said.

"They may not be, but any man charged with a crime deserves the best possible defense. It's not a lawyer's job to pre-judge them."

"It sounds like high morals and ethics, doesn't it?" I looked around at Hump.

"A good high sound to it," he said.

"Since I can't help you ..." He indicated the door with a nod of his head.

"Maybe you still can." I decided I might as well go ahead and run the flag up, and see how he reacted. "I know Ed Buddy hired you to handle it for them. How do I get in touch with him?"

"I don't think I know ..."

"Sure you do. He's from out of town. Chicago, I think."

He lowered his head and flipped some pages back toward the front of his address book. He lifted the book and held it toward me. "See? No Ed Buddy listed here."

"Maybe it's under his real name," I said.

It was just a flick off the top of my head, but I thought I saw it run home. The startled look on his face for just a brief second, and then covered over with a smoothness. He closed the address book with a loud bang and pushed it away from him. "I think you've wasted enough of my time."

"You thought it was a waste? I didn't." I winked at him and then walked to the doorway and picked up the paper bag. I dropped the oak club in it and rolled it up. "In fact, I really appreciate you seeing me."

"You realize I could have you arrested ..." He looked at the shattered phone. "... for forcible entry and assault?"

"Go ahead."

"Miss Forbes said your name was Jim Hardman. I assume you have an address, and the police will be able to find you?"

"I don't live on King's Court Road," I said.

Hump and I went out into the hallway and rang for the elevator.

"A waste of time," Hump said as we drove out of the parking lot.

"Not really."

"And maybe we've got cops looking for us right now."

"I doubt it," I said. "I think he's too busy kicking himself in the ass for the slip he made back there."

"About Ed Buddy's real name?" He got out a cigarette and held it unlit until I stopped for a red light. He drew on it and blew out a short puff of smoke. "What's that worth?"

"I'm not sure. Maybe nothing. Maybe something."

Hump hadn't been paying much attention to the direction I had taken. Now he looked around and recognized the neighborhood. "Where're we going?"

"Your place. Thought you might want to pack a bag."

"Good idea." He leaned back.

"And that Austrian shotgun the Cleveland fans gave you on Hump Evans Day."

"Why the shotgun?"

"I could say it's to keep the birds out of my garden."

"But the truth is …?"

"You win some and you lose some. I found out something back there. At the same time, we might have convinced somebody that we know enough to be dangerous."

Hump mulled that over in silence until I pulled up at the curb outside his apartment. He pushed the door open and looked over at me. "The next time you do me a favor, I wish you'd warn me ahead of time, so I could decide whether I want that favor."

"We forting up for the spring?"

He'd pushed the shopping cart through the aisles at Cloudt's while I piled in a few days' worth of groceries. I threw in everything from lox to a crown roast. At the end, I added a case of Michelob.

"Maybe."

"I see," he said. "You did it on purpose. You let them believe we knew something we don't, so they'd have to come out after us?"

"You've got to be kidding."

"You didn't?"

"I've been thinking about it ever since we left Hughes' office. I think it was a mistake, and now I'm scared shitless."

After we unpacked the groceries and stored the beer in the refrigerator, I checked the shotgun and loaded it. I propped it in the corner, near the doorway that led from the kitchen into the living room. Hump eyed the positioning and nodded.

The seed packages were still on the kitchen table. I sat down and spread them out in front of me. "You ever do any gardening, Hump?"

"A city boy like me?"

"While we're waiting for somebody to stop by and kill us, I thought I'd get the garden planted."

"Something to live after us, huh?" He grinned. "If it's that, I'd rather have a tree."

"We've got corn, two kinds of squash, butter beans and Chinese cabbage. No trees."

I left him looking over the seed packages and went into the bedroom. I dialed Marcy's number.

"Jim? I've been trying to reach you for more than an hour."

"We were out."

"We?"

"Hump's with me."

"Oh?" She paused. "Can you guess why I called?"

"How many guesses?"

"None. I found Ed Buddy in Joy Lynn's diary."

"What did you find out about him?"

"Not very much," she said. "At least it didn't tell me much about him."

"I'll come by for the translation."

"You don't have to," she said. "I'll drop them by. I've decided to work this afternoon."

"You get much sleep?"

"A couple of hours," she said.

"Sorry about that." Then, remembering, "About that Chinese cabbage...?"

"I thought it looked pretty."

"You want me to plant it?"

"No," she said. "I want you to frame it and hang it in the bathroom."

"Oooops." I waited a second. "We'll be back in the garden."

I dug the shallow hills and planted the two rows of summer squash. I was putting in the two rows of zucchini when Marcy came up the driveway and around the side of the house. Hump leaned the shotgun against the wall and stood up. She was dressed for the office, her hair pulled back tight and every hair in place. She was wearing a kind of mannishly-tailored pants suit and sensible heels. The diary was in one hand, with the pages of her translation stuffed in the center of it.

I waved at her, and went on and seeded the rest of the hills before I straightened up and stepped down from the terrace.

Marcy let me nuzzle her, and then she stepped away and looked at Hump's cast, the battered shape of his head and face, and the shotgun.

"Something's been going on?"

"Something," I said.

She placed the diary on the stone terrace wall. "I decoded every entry where Ed Buddy is mentioned."

"I appreciate it."

"I'll stop by on my way home," she said.

"I'd rather you didn't."

"What?" But her eyes slipped past me and saw the shotgun in a whole new way.

"It might get rough around here. You get a good night's sleep. I'll call you."

She didn't argue. I could see that she wanted to, but she choked it back. She reached up and I leaned down and kissed her. "Call me at six-thirty, if you can."

I watched her leave. I went back up and put in the second row of zucchini and covered them over. By the time I finished, it was lunch time, and we went down to the house and made some sandwiches and opened a couple of bottles of beer.

After I finished the sandwiches, I opened a second bottle of beer and carried the translations into the living room. I sipped at the beer and read through the decoded material twice.

*Feb. 7, 1973:* (Note from Marcy in the margin: "This is the first mention of Ed Buddy. The rest of the entry does not apply to him.")

*I found a new man tonight who might end up on my john list. His name is Ed Buddy and he told me he had recently moved to Atlanta from the midwest. He is forty or so but he is virile as a man half his age. And he seemed to like me and he said I turned him on.*

*April 2, 1973: An odd thing happened today. I was up early today because there was no work yesterday. Went shopping by myself. Looked in Davison's and Rich's but did not see anything I* liked. Went to Lennox Square to Saks. Saw a dress I liked but did not want to spend that much. I bought some make-up instead. Around lunchtime I drove by Harry's apartment. I just wanted to see if he was there. I saw Harry in the driveway in front of his duplex and Ed Buddy was talking to him. I don't understand how they know each other. I have put Ed on my john list. I don't know if I can ask Harry. He will be angry and he might think, because I know Ed Buddy's name, that I have been chipping on him. I will have to wait until the next time I see Ed.

April 4, 1973: Ed Buddy came by last night. It was chilly and slow on the street. As usual he was very nice and he took me to his suite at the Executive Motor Hotel. He calls it his hideout. He does not live there but he uses it as a business office. He has never told me what his business is. Afterwards, while I washed up and freshened my makeup, I asked him if he knew Harry. He said Harry who? And when I told him he said he did not know him. Then he asked me why I asked and I told him I thought I'd seen him talking to Harry the day before. He said it could not have been him because he had been out of the state the day before. I said I guess I'd made a mistake and it must have been somebody who was built like him.

April 6, 1973: Harry was in a bad mood last night. He came by just as Carol and I were about to leave for work. He said we were going to have to shake our asses a lot more. I said why? He said there are some bloodsuckers in town. What kind of bloodsuckers I wanted to know. A bloodsucker who is putting a head tax on all the girls. It was a hundred dollars a girl a week. I asked who this was and he said it was an out of town hood named Ed Buddy. Ed Buddy? I said. Harry asked if I knew him and I admitted I did and that I tricked with him now and then. About once a week. Harry said that he and some of the other players wanted to put it to Ed but they did not know how to reach him. So I told him about the suite Ed Buddy had at the Executive Motor Hotel after he said all they wanted to do was scare him so he'd give up the whole idea of *taking our money. He got excited and he was on the phone when Carol and I left.*

*April 7, 1973: Harry came to Sunday supper and I cooked fried chicken. Carol left right after supper to go to a double feature at the Hilan a few blocks away. I appreciated her leaving us alone. It was good to be alone with him and while we were in bed I asked him if they'd done anything about Ed Buddy. He said for me to forget about that completely. I asked him why and he said knowing too much could get me hurt. I asked why and he hit me in the back of the head and said because he had told me to. It didn't hurt that much but I cried for a time and he was gentle with me. He said it was for my own good and had he ever done anything that didn't have my best interest at heart. I said he hadn't and by the time Carol came back from the movies we were lovers again.*

*April 12, 1973: Something happened last night and I don't know what. Harry came by at midnight and picked me up. He was shaking and he said the attempt to teach Ed a lesson had not worked. Some people had been hurt and he thought Ed Buddy would try to find out who had sent the men after him. He said we ought to stay put and act like we didn't know anything. I said that would be easy because I didn't know anything. He said yes I did and that I had fingered Ed Buddy for them. And if he knew he was not going to like me for that reason. But I knew better.*

After the second reading I stuffed the decoded pages into the diary and hid it behind the cigar box in my closet. With Hump sitting shotgun, I went back up to the terrace and planted the rest of the garden, including the Chinese cabbage. After I wet the garden down with a thin coat of water, I looked around, and there was that mama cat taking a crap right where I'd planted the Chinese cabbage. Hump doubled up laughing, but I said, "Go ahead, fertilize the corn and the squash, too."

After a slow shower and another beer, I gave the decoded pages another reading. By that time, it was late enough to call Art.

# CHAPTER NINE

A rt dropped the large clasp envelope on the kitchen table and looked past me, toward Hump. "I think this is what you want, Jim." He continued to look at Hump, and Hump grinned and one-armed a bottle of beer for him. Art gulped at it and watched while I shook the contents out of the envelope. "Sooner or later," he said, "you're going to have to explain this to me."

"Later," I said.

"Sooner," he said.

"All right." I went into the bedroom and returned with the diary and the address book. "How are you at codes?"

I read the clipping from the *Atlanta Constitution* first. It was dated April 13, in the margin, with blue ballpoint ink.

### SHOOTOUT AT CITY MOTEL

A midnight shootout at the Executive Motor Hotel in downtown Atlanta last night led to the death of two unidentified men. The two men died in a hail of gunfire that rocked the parking lot and damaged a dozen cars parked there.

Robert Clemmons, a visitor from Sumter, S.C., said that he was in bed when he heard the first shot. 'I thought it was a backfire or a firecracker at first and then it turned into a full-scale war. I think it was shotguns and rifles and pistols all going at the same time.'

> A nearby car with the engine still run-
> ning and the doors open had been rented at
> Hartsfield International to a Randolph Carson
> of Kansas City, Missouri ...

I stopped reading the clipping and put it aside. Under it were a stack of police photographs of the parking lot after the shoot-out. One body was face-down on the asphalt, dark blood pooling around him. The cut-down, pistol-like grip of the sawed-off shotgun was near a clenched fist.

A series of photographs established the manner of death of the second man. A trail of blood which began about twenty feet from the car led to the driver's side. This man had probably been wounded at a distance from the car. He'd made it back to the car and collapsed. He'd been trying to crawl into the front seat when somebody stepped up behind him and blew off the top of his head. His knees were on the asphalt and his upper body lay across the front seat. It looked like he might have been praying.

The next exhibit was a copy of the official report of the investigating officer. It didn't tell me much that the newspaper and the pictures hadn't. It did stress the fact that the killer or killers weren't known. It was suggested that more than one man had been involved in the ambush. Shell casings found in one area of the parking lot led the police to believe that a .45 caliber submachine gun had been used, as well as a shotgun and pistols.

Art looked up from the diary with a puzzled look. "What the hell is this, anyway?"

"The Barrow girl's diary." I pulled out the decoded pages that Marcy had done for me the night before. "These are the sections that deal with Ed Buddy."

I gave him time to read it through. "Understand it now?"

"Where the hell did you ...?"

"Don't ask," I said. "Just be glad I got my hands on them, and be glad I've got a girl who's willing to spend all this time..."

"Ripped it off from the girl's apartment," he said, "and I'm supposed to be grateful?"

"The other thing," I said, handing him the address book, "is a john list she'd been putting together. Buddy's name is in there, but no address is given."

"What else did you steal from the apartment before you called me?"

"Nothing." I gathered the clipping, the official report and the photographs into a neat stack and shoved them back in the envelope. "Something's missing here. Two men killed in a parking lot the night before Carol and Joy Lynn get hit. You get makes on the dead men?"

"It wasn't pressing. Some hoods kill each other, so what? We had some people who thought it was a shootout over a drug shipment."

"But you got makes?"

"Sure we did," Art said. "Hours after the prints went off to Washington, we had the word on them. They were two medium-priced hit men, operating mainly in the Midwest until this time."

"The kind of money involved, it seems they might have afforded top talent," I said.

"Top talent wouldn't have made any difference."

"That bother you, too?"

"They got sold," Art said. "I've heard of professional hit men getting it while they're trying to get past a door, and I've heard of them missing and getting done in, but I've never heard of them not even getting across the parking lot."

"And the next day, Joy Lynn gets hers."

"Maybe Ed Buddy does some thinking after the shootout, and he decides Joy Lynn has been kissing and telling."

"And after Joy Lynn, this Buddy guy goes on and wastes Harry Falk, because he's involved too?"

Art gave me a thin smile. "It's certainly neat that way."

Art left with the diary and the address book and an explanation of how the code worked. I told him I wanted the diary back later, if that was possible. I wanted to read some more in it, so I could decide whether it ought to be passed on to Mr. Barrow. Probably not, but I wanted that option open.

"This bother you as much as it bothers me?" Hump had followed me into the bedroom. He sat on the edge of the bed while I knotted a tie and selected a light spring jacket.

"What?"

"The whole damned thing. Mostly it's this stud, Ed Buddy, if anybody really has a name like that. We've been running around him, and we don't know one damned thing about him.

"We know two," I said. "He's around forty, and virile as a man half his age."

"That's not a hell of a lot." For the first time, Hump realized I was getting ready to go out. "Where now?"

"Two stops. Come along if you want to. I want to see if I can find Willie Whitman, and I want to have a few more words with Wash Johnson."

"Willie know more than he told you the other night?"

"I didn't ask the right questions. And he's broke, and needs the call-back business."

"How does Willie look?" Hump asked.

"That farmer wiped the honest look off his face." I got the .38 P.P. out of the cigar box and stuffed it in my jacket pocket until I could store it in the glove compartment.

"And Wash Johnson?"

"Last time I talked to him, I didn't even know about Ed Buddy."

Hump took a few seconds to dig around in my stack of ties and settled on one that offended him less than the others. I tied it for him, and then we drove over to the Strip and parked on Peachtree Place. We walked in the direction of the Hollywood Bar. It was getting dark, and all down the street the hawkers were pushing the underground paper, *The Bird*, and the sex-ad magazine, *Dolls for Guys*.

We had a couple of beers before Willie came in. The bartender was the same one from the time before, and he asked me if I still had my woman under control. I told him some shit and tipped him a couple of times, and we were friends for life.

Willie saw us, and he was going to pass us by. I did my act and waved at him. "Hey, you remember me from the other night?"

He blinked at me. "Sure," he said, like he really didn't.

I wagged a finger at the bartender. "Beer for my friend here."

"I won't turn that down," Willie said.

After the bartender moved down the bar, Willie and Hump did their short nods that meant they knew each other. While Willie gulped at his beer, I leaned toward him. "I need something. It's worth a hundred."

"Ask," Willie said.

"Ed Buddy. I need to find him."

"Never heard of him."

"He's the one with the muscle who's pushing the pimps into line."

"In that case," Willie said, "I am now on vacation."

"You can ask around," I insisted.

"A hundred dollars won't buy a funeral."

"Two hundred then."

"I am back from vacation." Willie looked up at the clock over the bar. "Check back with me around eleven."

"Right."

"And I could use a ten in advance. Might have to buy a few beers while I'm asking around."

I got out a ten and tapped him on the leg with it. "Keep your head down. These people play with the rough side of the cob."

"I plan to."

I waved at the bartender and bought Willie another beer on our way out.

At 590 West, the seats on both sides of Wash Johnson were taken. He didn't see me. He was taking his usual long look down at the night streets. I let a waitress lead us to a table near the center of the club. We ordered J&B on the rocks and, while I waited for the drinks, I went over and tapped Wash on the shoulder. He looked up. He recognized me and frowned.

"Have a drink with my friend and me."

"I'm comfortable where I am," he said.

"I want to talk to you about a buddy of yours."

"Who's that?"

"Ed."

The bartender moved down to face me. I guess Wash was a tipper, and he didn't want Wash bothered. He was trying to decide whether I was annoying him enough to deserve the bouncer. Before he had time to decide, Wash got up and walked away from me. Behind us, the bartender put a glass with some ice cubes and some mix where Wash's drink had been on the bar, his way of saving the seat for him.

Wash heard the introduction of Hump but waved it aside. "What's this about? You could get us in a lot of trouble."

"The police know about Ed now."

"We know about the try on Ed that failed," Hump said.

"And the fact the two hookers got it because of that try," I said.

"What do you mean by that?"

"The Barrow girl fingered Ed, and he must have guessed it,"
I said.

"What do you want out of me?"

"A way to get to Ed. It's just a matter of time, anyway."

"He might not think that." Wash waved at the waitress and
ordered another Bloody Mary.

"How can I reach him?"

"I can't help you," Wash said.

"You're paying off, aren't you?"

"Hell, yes, I'm paying. After what happened to those two
girls, and then to Harry and that other girl, what would you do?"

"Then you must know how to get in touch with him."

The waitress brought Wash a Bloody Mary. He told her to put
it on his tab at the bar. He swirled the drink with the celery stalk
and then bit off an inch or so of it. "I don't get in touch with them.
They get in touch with me."

"How?" Hump asked.

"They call me, and they tell me where to meet them and when."

I leaned in. "Is it usually the same place?"

"Not usually. One time it was the bus station, and another
time it was the reference room at the downtown library."

"Who makes the pickup?"

"Both times it was a different guy. I put the envelope on the
table in front of me, and a guy comes in, says hello, and slides the
envelope toward him."

"How much is your payoff?"

"Four hundred." He shrugged his shoulders at me. "Now you
know I run four girls."

"When's the next one due?"

"It might be tomorrow. It might be the day after that."

"I want you to do something for me," I said.

Wash shook his head.

"As soon as you hear from them, I want you to call me and let
me know when and where the pickup is."

"I can't do that," he said.

"Come on, you know it's the best way."

"It's trouble for me," he said. "I could get dead."

Hump leaned in. "Four hundred a week for fifty-two weeks…that's a lot of money."

"Your girls are rolling their asses one night a week for him." I chewed on a chip of ice. "Just for him."

"You think I like it?"

"That must make a lot of points with your girls, too," Hump said.

Hump's remark sliced him some. The big thing a pimp has going for him is his balls. Take that from him, let his girls begin to doubt him, and he's just another john out there on the street.

"You have anything to do with the try on him at the Executive Motor Hotel?"

His head jerked up and he reached across the table and caught my forearm with a hand like a set of vise-grip pliers. "Jesus, don't you have any sense at all, Hardman? Talking like that?"

"Somebody must have taken up contributions to pay the two hit men," I said, "and if that happened, some of you had to donate."

"It wasn't me." He released my forearm, and I could feel the blood begin to flow again. "Not a nickel, not a dime, not a dollar."

"You expect me to believe that?"

"I didn't even know about it until it was over."

"Hard to believe that," I said.

"They might have tried, and couldn't reach me."

I shook my head at Hump and he laughed, a low rumble that made fun of the whole idea.

"Believe what you want to," Wash said.

"Drop that, for the time," I said. "You going to call me about the pickup?"

"Not a chance."

Hump looked down at his drink and then over at me. "The way I see it, Jim, we can trace it back to Ed Buddy in two ways."

"Tell me about them," I said.

"First of all, the way we're offering him right now. We can set up around Wash here, and watch the payoff and follow it back to him."

"That's the one I like," I said.

"It's got some drawbacks. You see, if we follow the man making the pickup, it might take quite a bit of time. He'll be doing a number of pickups, and the longer we have to follow him the more chance he'll have to spot us."

"The other one?"

"Wash'll think this one isn't friendly, and it's not." He took a deep breath and eased it out at Wash. "Right after I leave here, I go to Sport's Place and I talk to a couple of players I know. I say something about how I know that Wash Johnson organized the try on Ed at the Executive Motel, and how he contacted the hit men himself."

"You wouldn't do that," Wash said.

"The hell he wouldn't," I said.

"And then I'd make a few more stops, and drop the same handkerchief."

I nodded. "It's got good possibilities. We just watch Wash here until somebody punches his time clock for him, and then we follow them straight back to Ed."

"That's damned cold-blooded."

"That's the way it is," I said.

"It's a bluff," Wash said.

"I can drop the first handkerchief in half an hour. Maybe less than that." Hump pushed his drink toward the center of the table. "You going to call us, Wash?"

"You two aren't even human."

"Might be," Hump said, "but we don't sell ass by the pound, either."

"I'll think about it," he said.

I shook my head. "That's not good enough."

"You get to him, and he's going to know somebody set him up. I can't take that chance."

"He'll make a guess, but he won't be sure. Say he makes a dozen or twenty pickups on this day. Is he going to waste a dozen or twenty people to get the right one?"

"We bust him up, and it won't matter what he knows or what guesses he makes," Hump said.

"He can reach out of jail."

"He'll cut his losses. It won't be worth his time."

"All right." He dipped his head. "I'll call you."

"I'm in the book."

At the elevator, waiting, I looked back over to the bar. He was back at his regular seat, head angled away, looking down into the streets where his girls were. I think we'd broken his balls. We'd know in the next day or two.

⚜  ⚜  ⚜

At eleven, we reached the Hollywood after an hour or so of wandering around, wasting time. The bartender waved a hand at me, and I stopped and hooked a foot on the bar rail. "That little guy you bought a couple of beers for … I think he did himself in tonight."

"Huh?"

"Too much to drink. Two guys brought him in half an hour ago and put him in the back booth in the other room."

"You know the two guys?"

"Never saw them before," he said.

"I'll check on him." I went into the other room. The johns were in the far left corner. At one time there'd been a bowling machine, a couple of pinballs and a football. It turned out that winos didn't play the machines. Now there were just marks on the floor where the machines had been and a wide-open area, not used, and five booths against, the far wall. I could see Willie there, his head down on the table.

"Willie?" He didn't move. I edged into the seat next to him. My hand was on the seat and, before I got too far into the booth, I felt the sticky liquid. It could have been vomit, but it wasn't. I lifted my hand and looked at it in the bad light. It was like a black smear. I held the hand away from me and eased out of the booth. I leaned in and tried to find a pulse in Willie's neck. There wasn't one. His skin was cold, and he was getting rigid.

I went back to the bathroom. It had a rankness in it hard to believe. There wasn't any soap or towels. I rinsed the blood from my hand and dried it on a wad of toilet paper.

Hump was seated at the bar, a beer in front of him and a full beer and glass for me at the seat next to his. I waved at the bartender and he eased down the bar to me. "How was he doing when they brought him in?"

"Couldn't walk. His feet were dragging. That must be some load he put on. He must have put a touch on you."

"A buck or two," I said.

He grinned and moved away. Hump turned and looked at me. "What is it?"

"Willie ran out of cons." I reached into the scattering of change in front of him and located a dime. Taking the beer bottle with me, I went to the pay phone near the front entrance, called the police, and asked for Art Maloney's desk.

# CHAPTER TEN

The full, bright overhead lights were on in the back room of the Hollywood. It was probably the first time in a long time they'd been on at all. You could see the rainwater marks on the ceiling, and the half-hearted strokes the swamper had passed over the floor that morning.

They'd cleared away the customers and the gawkers and closed the bar for the night. The bartender and one wino who said he'd seen Willie being brought in were being questioned. I'd remained there long enough to hear their vague descriptions of the two men. They could have been anybody, or they could have been two of the hoods we'd had the brawl with. Maybe two of the studs who'd broken Hump's wrist.

Hump and I were seated in the back room, in the one next to the booth where I'd found Willie. We'd bought a couple of beers about the time the two cops from the street beat came in, and we'd talked to them some, but mostly we'd waited for Art to arrive. Now we were drinking the last of the beers, and we'd watched Willie being carted away. I'd felt bad about that, and it was going to take me a long time to get over the feeling that I'd sent Willie out to get himself killed.

Art came in from the front room and sat down across the booth from us. "So now you're getting people killed, huh?"

"He was supposed to ask around. He wasn't supposed to take them on single-handed." Art wasn't helping the bad feeling I had. Except for not giving a shit about farmers and taking them every chance he got, Willie had been a good guy. Except when he was hustling, he was straight down the line with you.

"You interested in how it happened?"

"Yeah."

"Doped-up whiskey or wine. He was knocked out but alive when they brought him in here. Sat him down in the booth behind us and stuck a few inches of knife in between his ribs five or six times."

I turned to Hump. "That means they knew we were meeting Willie here at eleven o'clock."

"A message to us," Hump said.

"You two are bothering somebody," Art said.

"Nothing like it's going to be."

"No use talking," Hump said. He spread his huge right hand on the table, palm down, ready to get up. "You know if Willie has any family?"

"I'll check around."

"Let us know. If you can't find any family, we'll put up for the funeral. All right with you, Hump?"

"Fine with me," Hump said.

"You're nice boys." I didn't miss the sarcasm in his voice. It would have been hard to. It was wet and dripping down his chin.

Two days passed. Slow days. The hardest kind of time to do, the waiting time. Marcy came by the first night and fixed the crown roast. I found time to drop by the hardware store on Highland and bought three dozen tomato plants. I spent a cool twilight putting them in, watched by the mama cat, who stretched out on the terrace wall, sleepy-eyed and waiting her turn.

On the morning of the third day, Wash Johnson called. The call was brief and to the point. "Pickup's in the reference room of the library on Carnegie Way. Same as the time before. Twelve noon today."

"Got it," I said.

"You better cover me."

"You're covered."

"I mean it."

"My word."

I rang off and called Art. I think I caught him with one knee on the bed.

Even with the short notice, we had it set up and ready by eleven-fifteen. Wash Johnson probably wouldn't arrive until a few minutes before the pickup. We went ahead and built a box around the library, inside and out. Because there was a chance the pickup man might be one of the four who'd seen Art, Hump and me, we arranged it so that our heads were down.

I was in the second level of stacks at the rear of the reference room, hidden by a thick shelf of books. I had a good sightline with Art's man, who was behind the reference desk. He seemed to have the best job of all. He wasn't doing anything but brushing hips with a couple of well-built librarians and, every minute or so, looking up at me.

Carnegie Way is a two-way street. It would have been easier if it had been one-way. As it was, Art had to cover both possibilities. Art and Hump were in a car that pointed down Carnegie Way toward the Davison parking lot. Another car, staffed by plainclothes men, headed in the direction of Forsyth Street and Margaret Mitchell Square.

At ten of twelve, after I'd read the same page of a book on genetics about ten times without understanding any of it, Wash Johnson came in and took one of the front tables, near the reference desk. He had dressed for it like a real dude. Blue blazer and cream-colored slacks and white shoes. Art's man noticed him and looked up at me. I nodded. My part was done. I remained just a moment longer, and saw Wash take a narrow brown envelope from the inside pocket of the blazer. He placed it on the table in front of him. I left the stacks then, hurried to the elevator, and took it to the basement level. There was a door there, kept locked most of the time, that led to Forsyth Street. I left by that door and crossed Forsyth on a dead run. I entered the Dunkin' Donut Shop on the triangular point that separates Forsyth and Peachtree. I sat at the end of the counter near the window and ordered a milk and a chocolate honey-glazed. While I sipped the milk and ate the donut, I turned in my seat and watched the front of the library. I had a good view of Carnegie Way and the two stakeout cars.

At twelve, exactly, a car pulled up in front of the library and a fat teenage girl got out and waddled up the steps under the weight of about fifteen books. Unlikely. She proved me right by coming down the steps a minute later, arms empty now and no envelope in sight. Other cars passed but none stopped, and there was the steady noon traffic of people walking in and out of the library. I finished the donut and ordered another chocolate honey-glazed. When I turned back to the window, I realized that we hadn't boxed it in completely, that we'd missed it, or they'd changed the rules on us. I knew that when I noticed the man. He'd come from my blind side, from down Forsyth, and now he stopped on the sidewalk outside my window. There wasn't a crosswalk there, and he waited his time and found an opening in the traffic. As he stepped off the curb, I saw the bulge high on his right hip. It could have been one of those huge wallets, but I didn't think so. And then the seersucker jacket settled over the bulge like it had been tailored that way, and he reached the other side of the street and walked the thirty yards or so and up the steps into the library.

I finished the milk and took the partly eaten donut outside with me. The only vehicle parked on this side of Forsyth was a truck unloading at the back of Brooks Brothers. That meant he'd probably walked. I moved away from the donut shop and toward the point of the island, where the newspaper boxes were. I leaned on one of the boxes and watched the front of the library. Three or four minutes after he entered, the man in the seersucker jacket came out again. I fished out a dime, leaned over the *Constitution* box, and got out a paper. When I looked around again he was at the curb near the corner, ready to cross to the narrow concrete island where I was. Behind him, just coming out of the library and stopping on the steps, Art's man from behind the reference desk nodded toward the man in the seersucker jacket and lit a cigarette. That was the established signal.

I had one more look at him, this time closer and full front face. It was a bland, round face with a pencil-line mustache out of some 1930's movie. It was a quick glance, because he was angling toward me. He wasn't going back up Forsyth. I put my back to him and stepped out. I hit a seam in the traffic and crossed Peachtree. I was fairly sure that somebody from one of the stake-out cars would be tailing him. If I played it right, I could head him and we'd have him boxed in, front and back. The chase running a distance, we could switch off occasionally and give him something new to look at now and then.

I hesitated on the other side of the street and looked into the window of the novelty shop there. I got enough of his reflection in the glass to see that he was coming on. I made a slow turn and walked toward Peachtree and Ellis. I was about twenty yards ahead of him and I tried to maintain that interval. The light was red at Ellis and it looked like I might lose it, but at the last moment the light changed and I kept going. I passed Bailey, Banks and Biddle, and I was in front of Woolworth's before I risked a look over my shoulder. The man in the seersucker suit wasn't there.

Art Maloney was. He gave a nod toward the S&W cafeteria, and pushed through one of the revolving doors and went inside. I turned into Woolworth's, fished out some change, and took my time buying a pack of cigarettes at the machine near the window. I was lighting one when Art passed outside the window and nodded at me. I put my back to the window and counted to ten. When I turned around, the man in the seersucker jacket was passing. I let him get a few paces on me and then I went back outside. I remained twenty feet behind him, trying to keep a few shoppers between the man and me. Beyond him, now and again, I'd get a flash of Art. He was the head now and I was the tail, and I guess the man in the seersucker could be called the dog's body.

At Cain, the man crossed the street and stopped, turning left, waiting for the light to change. He was going to cross Peachtree again. Art kept going, heading toward Peachtree Center. There wasn't much else he could do. I saw him in time and didn't cross Cain. I turned and waited for the same light to change. When it went green, we stepped off the curb about the same time, Cain Street separating us, and headed for the other side of Peachtree. Along the way, a horde of women shoppers edged up on me, and I let them gain on me and finally surround me. It was good cover and, when I glanced over at the man we were tailing, he didn't seem aware of me at all.

I reached the other corner, the construction site where they had torn down the old Henry Grady Hotel and were getting started on the new Peachtree Plaza Hotel. The pickup man continued straight down Cain, toward Spring. I looked up Peachtree and saw that Art had stopped, but he wasn't coming back yet. It was up to me. The light changed, and I started across Cain. I was about halfway across when a car making a left onto Cain honked at me. I turned and saw Hump in the back seat of one of the unmarked cars. He shook his head at me and I stopped and let him make the turn. Then I crossed over and stopped. Far down the block, the pickup man was heading for the bus station. The car with Hump in it passed him near the corner of Spring. The car eased to a stop near the curb and Hump got out. A coat folded over his arm hid the cast.

Art was at my elbow. "Hump's got him," I said.

The pickup man crossed Spring and went into the bus station. Hump was almost shoulder-to-shoulder with him. Art and I took our time getting there. When we reached the bus station, the unmarked car was still there. Art got into the front seat next to the driver. I stripped off my jacket and tie and tossed them through the open window into the back seat. "Watch those for me."

"Is that supposed to be a disguise?" Art asked.

"According to the Arco book on how to be a detective, it is," I said.

I was going in after him, but I didn't have to. The pickup man came out, pushing past without looking at me. He was carrying a black leather attaché case now. Hump was right behind him. He stopped beside me and we watched him head back up Spring, the attaché case banging against the side of his leg.

"He got the case from one of the lockers and put a couple of envelopes in it," Hump said.

"Collecting's over for the day," I said. "Might have made a number of trips here to the bus station, each time dropping off a couple of the payoffs. Didn't want to be caught with the whole load on him."

We moved out to the curb. The unmarked police car with Art and the driver in it kicked over and headed down Cain. They would take the first left they could and work their way over to Spring. Hump and I let the pickup man have a half-block, and then I led off. Hump stayed half a block behind me. After a block or so, I stopped and looked into a store window and Hump moved up and took the lead. We leapfrogged that way for three or four blocks, and then I started getting nervous. I knew the area well enough to know there were a number of small parking lots scattered about, and I made my guess that he was heading for one of them. There still wasn't any sign of Art and the car, and that bothered me. If he didn't show soon, we might lose the pickup man and the tag home.

It started to blow apart. Hump was tailing the man and I was drifting a good distance back. Suddenly, the man turned and looked down the street, directly at Hump. I'd seen the turn coming and was able to ease into a doorway. Hump was in the open and couldn't do much more than he did. He looked at the pickup man and looked away. He was a few steps from a side street to his right. He kept on going for those few steps, then he turned and went down the side street.

It was up to me now, and I didn't like it. The man was jumpy now. Maybe he had a feeling. It was like that, sometimes. The only hope I had was that the pickup man, now that Hump was gone, would fall back into his original pattern. He'd think he'd been wrong about Hump tailing him, and he'd tell himself that he was just getting jumpy.

I counted to fifteen and stepped out of the doorway. It looked like luck was with me. He'd turned and walked on. He was about a full block or more ahead of me now, and I'd have to make it up somehow. I set out at a brisk walk. I needed some cover. I felt naked, guts out and wrapped around my neck, but there wasn't anything I could do about it. Art had failed us and, if we were going to lose him, I wanted to be sure that I was close enough to get the tag numbers off his car.

I'd made up half the distance between the man and me when he turned off the sidewalk and went out of sight. That probably meant there was a parking lot beyond the building ahead. I had to get closer before he pulled out, so I set out at a lope. I reached the far end of the building, stopped, and put my back to it, still not looking past it. I tried to ease my breath, and felt around in my pocket for a scrap of paper. I found an old deposit slip and uncapped my pen.

I heard the engine kick over and it seemed very close, next to the wall of the building. I started to move away, heading toward a doorway about twenty yards away, but the black Buick nosed past the end of the building and stopped on the sidewalk ramp. The rear door swung open. I looked inside and saw the nose of a .38 pointed at me, held in the hand of the pickup man.

"Come here."

I played it dumb. "Who? Me?"

"You," the man said. "Unless you want it on the street."

I stepped into the Buick and didn't touch the car door.

"Close the door," the man said.

I pulled it closed. As I did, I looked in the front seat and saw two of the bruisers from the fight at the Book Store Bar. One was the stud with the bad throat, the one that I'd handled. He was in the front passenger seat. The driver was the one that Hump had hit first and put out of the fight early.

"Yeah," the one with the bad throat croaked at me, "it's me."

The Buick pulled out, down the sidewalk ramp and into the street. It turned right and moved off at a good clip.

"Don't you know all that walking might be good for your heart and still bad for your health?" The pickup man grinned at me.

The two in the front seat laughed. The one with the bad throat said, "This time you didn't bring a chair with you."

I turned and looked at him and, when I did, the pickup man pushed me forward and hit me in the back of the head with the flat side of the .38. It hurt like hell and it dazed me, but it didn't put me completely out. But I acted like it did and I went limp, and he pushed me onto the carpeted floorboards and put a foot on the back of my head.

# CHAPTER ELEVEN

Playing possum wasn't all that it's cracked up to be. It didn't take long for me to find that out. I'd got a few less lumps from the side of the .38. That was the credit side. On the debit side, there I was, face down on the floorboards, with the weight of the pickup man's foot on the back of my head and neck. It Was uncomfortable, and the shoe seemed to weigh about twenty pounds.

"Hardman," the one with the bad throat croaked. "They ought to call him Softman."

"He ruined you," the driver said.

"You see it?"

"No," the driver admitted.

"Of course you didn't. You were flat on your ass out the whole time, that's why."

"I got told about it."

"That's the only way you'd know," Bad Throat said. There was a shifting of weight in the front seat. "How's our boy doing?"

"Bleeding on the upholstery," the pickup man said.

About twenty minutes after they'd picked me up on Spring Street, the Buick braked and the pickup man lifted the shoe from the back of my neck. "Sit up, Hardman."

I got my hands under me and pushed myself up. I sat on the seat next to the pickup man. I was too close to him, so he wagged the .38 at me and I moved away another foot or so.

"Nothing fancy," the pickup man said.

The nose of the Buick was pulled up at the back of a weathered old building, almost touching a concrete ramp. I used the hand away from the pickup man and tugged at the collar of my shirt. It was stuck to my neck hair with dried blood. "Where are we?"

"Out near the graveyard," Bad Throat said.

"That's your best rip today," the driver said. "Out near the graveyard."

The pickup man opened the door on his side. "You going to come in nice and easy, or do you want it the hard way?"

"I'll walk it," I said.

"That's a good boy," the pickup man said.

"Good? He's a fucking sweetheart," Bad Throat said. "The next best thing to pussy."

The pickup man eased out of the car and stood waiting, while I inched my way over to the door and stepped out. As soon as I was clear of the car, I blinked up at the sky. It was clouding over, like we might be getting a good spring rain. Good for my garden, with the tomato plants in and the seeds waiting. But, as Hump had said, maybe I should have planted a tree.

"Up there."

The direction was wasted. Bad Throat and the driver each took an arm, and they ran me up the steps and onto the concrete ramp. When we reached the door, they rammed me against the wall and held me there while the pickup man unlocked a big Yale and pushed the door open. Now he was carrying the attaché case he'd picked up at the bus station. "I'll get the light."

They held me in the open door while the pickup man crossed the dark room. It was an odd odor, a room full of conflicting smells. The scent of dust and something else. I grabbed at it and picked the bones, and I got it just before the light went on. It was the smell of flour.

I understood the smells then. It was an old bakery that hadn't been used for years. To the left, I could see the floor marks where the ovens had been, and the capped-off gas lines near the wall. Along the right wall were four large stainless steel mixing units with the dough hooks still attached. A couple of long, wood-topped tables were in the center of the room. And here and there, high cooling racks on wheels. Beyond the tables, I could see the only additions this crew had made to the room: a canvas folding cot and a couple of straight-backed chairs.

The pickup man placed the attaché case on one of the tables. "I'm going to call Ed from down the street. He might want to talk to our boy here."

"How long'll you be gone? I could use a beer." Bad Throat walked me across the room, around the tables, and stopped near the cot.

The pickup man shook his head. "Not sure. I might have to pick Ed up and bring him here."

"No sweat," Bad throat said. "We got the sweetheart here to keep us company."

"Watch the case for me." The pickup man tapped the attaché case with his knuckles and went out, closing the door after him. He didn't even look at me, and that sent a shiver down me. The driver reached back under the tail of his coat and brought out a short-barreled .38. He sat down in one of the chairs and rested the pistol on his knee.

Bad Throat seemed to be waiting for something. When it came, the Buick's engine starting up, he turned and smiled at me. "Sweetheart, you made me look bad the other night."

"Reamed your hole, the way I heard it," the driver said.

I didn't say anything. Nothing I could say would make any difference.

"Cops and ex-cops make me sick. Puking sick." Bad Throat held out a hand to the driver. "You got the tape?"

The driver reached into his coat pocket and brought out a thick, one-inch-wide roll of white adhesive tape.

"Turn around, sweetheart. Wrists together flat, no space between them."

I did as he said. I tried to keep some space between the wrists, but after he looped the first layer of tape around my hands he pressed the wrists together. Another dozen or so loops, and it was done. He caught me by the shoulder and turned me. He placed the roll of tape on the table, next to the attaché case.

"Remember, Ed might want to talk to him," the driver said.

"I ain't going to hurt him," Bad Throat said. "I'm just going to dust him off." He held up his left fist so I could see the depressed, busted knuckles. "You made me look bad, and I didn't like that at all."

While I was looking at his left, he ducked his shoulder and swung the right at me. I guess I'd been expecting it, and I tried to turn and take part of it on my hip. I didn't get turned far enough, and I took the force of it in my left side. I fell back across the cot and against the wall. After the first shock, it felt like somebody had reached a hand into a hole in my side and torn a section of my guts out.

"That's enough," the driver said.

"Shut up!" Bad Throat leaned over me. "Sweetheart here likes it. He likes to show how tough he is." He grabbed me under the arms and was pulling me to my feet. His face was close to mine, and I thought, why the shit not? I was going to get my ass kicked, and being passive wasn't going to make it hurt any less. "Tell him how tough you are."

I jerked my head forward and butted Bad Throat across the nose. He threw me against the wall and straightened up. As he stepped back, I took a kick at his groin and missed, hitting the inside of his right knee instead. "Sonofabitch!" Spit peppered my face, and he leaned toward me and clubbed me on the side of my head.

"Not in the head," the driver said. "Ed might want to talk to him."

"You see what he just did to me?"

"Not in the face," the driver said.

I turned my head back and looked at Bad Throat. His eyes were watering, and he ran a hand across his face. A thin smear of blood covered the lower part of his face. He looked at the blood in his hand. "Now you've done it. Now you've goddam tore it."

It was good as over then. I knew I was done. He worked me over from my knees to my shoulders. When the pain was bad enough, I told myself to go ahead and black out, but it wasn't that easy. I remained in a kind of twilight, and the blows seemed to run together until I thought he had about ten hands. It went on and on, and I didn't believe it when the grunting stopped.

"Enough," the driver said. "That's enough."

"He's all yours," Bad Throat said.

I think it was the driver who lifted me and stretched me out on the cot. I felt my legs being pulled together and, from the tightness down there, I knew that the driver had taped my ankles together.

"I worked up a thirst," Bad Throat said. He seemed to be about a mile away. "I'm going down the street to get a six-pack."

"Virg might be back in a second," the driver said. "If he didn't have to pick up Ed."

"Fuck him."

The light went out. I could hear the footsteps. "The dust is getting to my sinus," the driver said. "I'll wait for you outside. He ain't going anywhere."

"Whose hole got reamed this time?"

"His," the driver said.

"Fucking-aye," Bad Throat said.

The door closed after them.

It was dark in the room and I was choking on blood or vomit and I couldn't sit up. I didn't know if an hour had passed or a day.

I tried to turn my head. I wasn't fast enough. It came out sour and lumpy. It spilled across the cot and ran down across me, soaked up by my shirt and my hair. I couldn't stand that, and the energy came from somewhere. I rocked the cot and it tipped over, and I fell on the concrete floor. I took most of the fall on my shoulder and just stayed there, waiting to see if the pain would go away. It didn't. I didn't think it ever would, and I let myself moan once, to see if that would help. It came out louder than I meant it to, and I clenched my teeth to shut it off.

Foxy. Got to be foxy. But how? Hands in back. Not much I can do with them that way. Try to work them around in front? Maybe. Had Bad Throat made a mistake? Maybe. So eager to beat the crap out of me. Otherwise he should have taped the hands together higher up. Maybe even pulled the elbows together and taped them. Screw you, Bad Throat, you're not that smart.

Still on my side, I drew my knees up, trying to get them against my stomach. Too much stomach. Worry about that later. First things first. Got to work my hands down and get them past my rump. The first part is easy, half way there, but I can feel the arms pulling out of the sockets. Just one more pain. Think about the other ones. There. Hands past my rump. Now slide them up the thighs. One more push. Over the shoes. The edge of the leather heels tearing at my wrists. But it is done. My hands are in front of me. Screw you, Bad Throat.

The next thing next. Got to sit up and try to work on the tape the driver wrapped around my ankles, over my socks. Easier than I thought, just turn on my back, put the hands over my knees and pull myself up. There. Hands feeling for the end of the tape. I can't find it. The desperation is coming on, the scream of frustration in the back of my throat. Can't do that. Take a deep breath. Then another. Try again, the fingernail tracing the tape. Looking for the rough line of the end. Maybe. Here. The slow, precious time to work the fingernail under the tape. Enough to lift it. Enough to unwrap it. The socks coming

PIMP FOR THE DEAD

apart as I peel the tape away. Then the end, and the legs sprawl apart.

And now the next thing next. I crawled across the floor to the nearest table. I put my hands on the edge of the table and try to pull myself up. The arms don't like it, and the rest of my body doesn't either. The second try I make it, but as soon as I am upright the knees give out on me and I fall across the table. The attaché case hits me in the chest. Another pain. But something else. A rattle. Something in the table rattled.

I wait until the legs stop shaking. Thinking about the rattling I heard. Not the table falling apart. Sounds more like the rattling of silverware in a drawer. The time, the time is running away. Can't get this close and let them catch me again. I use a shoulder to brace myself on the table and my hands to move below the table top. I go almost all the way around the table before I find it. A wide, metal-fronted drawer. It opens easily, like it is on rollers. Careful now, warning myself. My hands working a puzzle in the dark. Parts and pieces I don't recognize. Feeling the rust come off on my hands. About to give up when I feel the wooden handle. I lift it carefully and place it on the table top. I trace the length of it, the blade and the edge with the roughness of pits and rust.

At first, I try to hold the handle in my fingertips and saw against the tape. Not much progress at first, and I push harder. The blade slips out of line and cuts my wrist. My god, no, not a vein. I put the knife on the table and lift the cut wrist to my mouth. I taste the cut. Not a vein, after all. A shallow out, bleeding but not gushing.

Got to try something else. Might not be lucky the next time. Maybe the drawer. I push it until it's almost closed. I hold the knife by the blade and place it on the top edge of the drawer. Then, slowly, I close the drawer. The knife holds in place. I jam the drawer as hard as I can. The knife is locked in tight. I bend over and saw against the blade, the tape tearing as much as cutting, sweating and grunting with the effort, until the tape parts.

I tear away hair and all, maybe some skin, and then my hands are free. Too much time has passed. I don't like the way time has passed. It looks like they would check on me. Unless they think I am half dead. Unless they are sitting back on that ramp, drinking cool beer and watching the spring coming. Maybe the coolness of the spring rain, if the rain came.

Free now, and I have a weapon. I do not like the knife. I don't understand how people can use them. But a knife is better than nothing, and I pull the drawer open and take the knife with me. Still not satisfied. I'd like some other weapon. I walk around the room, looking for something that I can use for a club.

The stainless steel mixing machines, the bowls, and the huge dough hooks. I miss them the first circuit of the room. On the second, I reach down and shake the dough hook on the first machine. It is locked in. It would take a spanner wrench to free it. I try the second machine. The same. But the third dough hook wobbles, and I kneel on the floor and pull at it. It comes free and falls into the bowl with a loud clang. I get to my feet and lift the dough hook out of the bowl. It is a wicked piece of equipment. About a yard long, with a heavy slotted handle. It thins as it moves away from the handle, curving and becoming a half-moon. It is stainless steel and weighs nine or ten pounds.

Swinging it, getting used to it, I carry it to the doorway. I lean against the doorway. The door opens outward, I remember that. I move away until I'm flat against the wall. Now I will see if I can muster some strength. My legs feel better now. Now I wait. Now.

The door swung open, the light a narrow sliver in the darkness, and I can hear them, a bit of the beer loudness in their voices.

Bad Throat said, "… how sleeping beauty is now, after his workout?"

"Wore out," the driver said, "plenty wore out."

They came through the doorway together. After a couple of steps, the driver stopped. "Get the light, smart-ass," he said. I flicked my eyes at him. He was standing just inside the door, relaxed, a tall can of beer in one hand and a full 6-pack under his arm. Ahead of him, Bad Throat was walking carefully, not yet accustomed to the darkness.

"Yooohooo," Bad Throat called, "how is Hardman now?"

I couldn't wait. It had to happen now, if it was going to happen. I stepped away from the wall and swung the dough hook at the driver in a kind of two-handed tennis backhand. The hook caught the driver across the chest and almost tore him in half, throwing him back against the doorframe. The open can of beer kicked up and splattered against the wall. I didn't wait to see him fall. There wasn't time. Bad Throat was slow, but he was beginning his turn. I was on him before he got around. The first swing of the dough hook didn't land where it-was supposed to. The strength in my arms failed me, and the hook dipped low and hit Bad Throat across the hips. There was enough steam left to hurt him, and he doubled over, screaming with the pain. I lifted the dough hook and brought it down, aiming for his head and missing it, and knew that I'd broken his collarbone. He was falling then, and I hit him and hit him and hit him, until he was face down on the floor. The edges of his rubber shoe soles squeaked on the concrete for a time, and that was all.

I turned on the light. I looked at the bloody work I'd done and threw the dough hook across the room. It clanged against one of the stainless steel mixing bowls. I put my head down on one of the wooden tables and counted up to sixty twice. That was all the rest I could allow myself if the pickup man was still expected. I pushed myself up from the table and spent the next ten minutes cleaning up the mess I'd made.

I sat in a chair beside the door. I had the 6-pack of tall Bud at my feet, the .38 I'd taken from the driver, and a .45 automatic that Bad Throat had been carrying. Ready and waiting. I picked up the 6-pack and pulled a can out of the plastic webbing. It blew when I popped the tab. The beer felt cool in my face, so I lifted the beer and poured the rest of it over the top of my head. It was better to smell like beer than vomit.

I drank part of the second beer. When I threw that can away I started dozing, and I had to get to my feet and walk around the room. Maybe they weren't coming, and I was a fool to wait for them. I might make it to a phone if I tried. If anyone would let me use their phone after they got a look at me, and a smell.

No, I'd wait.

It seemed like hours. Hours and hours.

I heard the sound of the car engine, and stood up. This was followed by the flat clap of car doors slamming shut. More than one door. That meant the pickup man wasn't alone. Ed Buddy... maybe he came along for that talk with me. Rasp of grit under shoes on the ramp. Coming close. They didn't have to unlock the Yale this time. The door swung open. The first man through the doorway I thought I didn't know. The second man was the pickup man, the seersucker jacket wrinkled and baggy now.

The pickup man said, "What the hell, Ed?"

I aimed past the pickup man's shoulder and put a round from the .45 into the doorframe. Both of them whirled to face me before they turned to stone.

After I got their iron and threw it out the door, I stood in the doorway and looked out at the nose of the black Buick. I couldn't think of any reason why I shouldn't, so I lifted the .45 and sighted in. I put three rounds through the windshield.

# CHAPTER TWELVE

"Sure you know him," Art said. He was leaning over me, trying to get the .45 out of my hand, and doing it carefully so he wouldn't get a round in the leg or the foot. I'd given up the .38 without any trouble, but now, for some reason, I didn't want to release the big Army issue automatic. "Think back, a few nights ago."

I blinked. I was having trouble keeping my eyes open. And my brains felt scrambled and fried hard. "I can't."

"I need this." He tugged at the .45.

"Huh?"

"Ballistics test," he said.

That must have touched an old button, from years back. I turned the hand palm up, and he lifted the gun out with the tips of his fingers. Behind me, standing behind my chair, Hump let out a long breath and dropped his hand from my shoulder.

"Sure you do," Hump said. "This is one who likes to do his own rough work." He took a couple of steps toward the two of them, the pickup man and the one I guessed was Ed Buddy. Both had their hands cuffed behind them, and they were watching me with a casual disinterest. "The other night, at the Book Store Bar, he squared off against Art."

Click. That was the one. The stud who looked like a TV insurance pitchman until you saw the eyes. The dead man behind the face. "Ed Buddy? Is that your name?"

"One of them," he said.

I looked past him, around the bakery. An ambulance had carted the driver and Bad Throat away a few minutes before. They'd wanted to take me, too, but I said I'd come later, after I'd talked to Art.

It had been a hairy few minutes. The police cruiser had pulled up next to the black Buick about five minutes after I shot out the windshield. They'd come to investigate reports of gunfire. For a time, it had been a standoff. They'd wanted me to throw out my guns, and I said I wasn't going to. It looked like I might get shot or have to shoot a cop. But one of them had a cool head, and I convinced him to call the department and talk to Art. Art must have burned some hide off them, because right after that they came in nice as could be, and handcuffed the pickup man and the man I now knew to be Ed Buddy. They said nothing about me giving my guns up.

One of the young policemen was still in the room, standing over next to the handcuffed men. The other one rushed in while I was getting my head together enough to recognize Ed Buddy from the brawl. He'd been sent down the street to get me some kind of shirt and a couple of wet towels. Hump took the shirt from him, ripped off the plastic cover, and began unbuttoning it. I took the wet towels, barely warm, and scrubbed off my face and neck and hair. It helped some, but I could still smell the vomit. Either there was some still in my hair, or I had the scent of it caught far back in my nostrils and it would take time for it to wear away.

I stood up and stripped off my shirt and t-shirt. There was blood and vomit and beer on both of them. I turned the towels inside out and washed again, head to waist.

Ed Buddy watched me, eyes dull and glazed. "Any reason why we have to stay here and watch his topless show? I'd rather be in jail."

"What's your rush?" Art asked.

"I want to make my one call," Buddy said.

Hump helped me with the shirt. It was a tight fit. I had to suck in my gut to get it buttoned. But it had the new smell, and that warred with the vomit.

"I've got a question for you," I said. "Why'd you kill Joy Lynn Barrow and the dwarf girl? Because she fingered you?"

"I didn't kill her."

"That's hard to believe."

"Believe what you want to. You cops and ex-cops do that anyway. Anything to tie it up all neat." He dipped his head and spat, about an inch or so away from the young cop's shiny black shoe. "I liked that girl and she liked me, and I wouldn't have killed her."

"How about the two hit men in the motel parking lot? You like them, too?"

Ed Buddy shook his head and looked away.

"How about Harry Falk, and the hippie girl with him?"

He shrugged.

"How about Willie Whitman?"

"Who's he?"

"An old con man down on his luck. Sold information for a living."

Ed Buddy looked over at Art. "I don't want to answer any questions. I want to call my lawyer."

"Anybody we know?"

"Denton Hughes."

"That's what I figured."

The two young cops took them out to the paddy wagon. Hump walked over and lifted the dough hook from beneath one of the mixing machines. "This the tool?"

"Jawbone of an ass," I said.

I spent the night and all of the next day at Grady Hospital. It rained sometime during the night, or all the night. I wasn't sure.

I was sedated part of the time, and I kept waking up and hearing it on the window. Hump was with me part of the time, and once I woke up and Marcy was leaning over me, crying and wetting my pillow. And there were some vague moments when I thought that Art was in the room. He was trying to explain how they'd lost me on Spring Street. It had something to do with a street that was blocked when they started to do their little box step around to pick us up. I think he said it was the gas company putting in a new gas line. They'd been blocked, not able to move forward, but not able to back out, either. And by the time they'd located Hump they couldn't find me, and they knew I'd been tailing too close and had been grabbed. Sorry, but they'd done the best they could.

Confused, the memories warped. But the dough hook was real.

❧ ❧ ❧

Art came by the next afternoon. He was still dizzy from lack of sleep, and he slumped into a chair next to my hospital bed.

"How you feel?"

I forgot and tried to shrug. I decided that talking didn't hurt that much. "I'll be all right after the black and blue goes away." I put out two fingers and he put a smoke in them and lit it for me. "How're you doing with Ed Buddy?"

"Putting it together, bit by bit."

"How does it look?"

"The .45 you took off the guy you almost killed ... slugs from it match the ones we took out of the hit man who died half in his car and half out of it. That gives us a lever on him, and he's beginning to chip around the edges." He shook his head at me. "I wish you hadn't come so close to killing him."

"It seemed the thing to do at the time," I said. "Sorry."

"Well, he's tough, and alive enough to be scared. I've got a man out at an apartment on Peachtree Road that he told us about. There's supposed to be a .45 caliber submachine gun out there, also used in the same brushfire war with the two hit men."

"That doesn't touch Ed Buddy."

"Funny thing about him. Has a big-time lawyer who tried to spring him. Seemed surprised that the judge wouldn't set bail."

"What you got him for?"

"So far, kidnapping you off the streets of Atlanta."

"Me?"

"Sure. And that ought to keep him around until we tie some of the rest of this mess to him."

"Kidnapping? Me?" I forgot myself again and laughed. Art stayed just long enough to watch my eyes water from the pain. Then he grinned at me and left.

Hump and Marcy checked me out of the hospital that evening, and I was still so shaky that they put me to bed at my house and fed the mama cat and left me alone. During the night I woke up sweating and shivering, and I got out of bed and went into the kitchen and got down the half-bottle of armagnac that I had left over from the winter. I had a good belt, and opened the large brown envelope that was on the kitchen table with my name on it. There was also a note on it in Marcy's handwriting. *Art said you could have this back.* I opened the clasp and shook the diary, the address book, and the sheets of paper with the decoding on them out on the table. I had another drink, and then I put Joy Lynn's personal life aside without looking at it again. I drank about half the armagnac, and then I fell into bed and slept like a drunk.

The phone rang about nine the next morning. I was in the bathroom, trying to tear the foil from a pack of Alka-Seltzer. I let the phone ring on until I dropped the tablets into the half-glass of water. I carried the glass with me, sat on the edge of the bed, and picked up the receiver.

"Mr. Hardman, this is John Barrow."

I gulped some of the fizz and said good morning.

"Mr. Maloney from the Atlanta police called me yesterday."

I said I was glad he had, because I hadn't been in much shape to do anything the day before.

"I'm coming to Atlanta this afternoon, and I thought I'd drop by to see you, if it's all right with you. I want to know exactly what happened."

I said I'd be glad to see him.

"And I want a favor from you. The sheriff... Hubie King... said you might be able to arrange it so I could see the man who killed Joy Lynn."

"I don't know about that." I held the phone aside and drank the rest of the Alka-Seltzer. "I won't do it if you've got any idea of starting trouble."

"I just want to look at him," Barrow said. "I'm not even sure I have anything I want to say to him."

"With those ground rules, I might be able to do something."

He thanked me, and said he'd be in Atlanta about four in the afternoon.

❖  ❖  ❖

Around two in the afternoon, I was heating a can of soup when it came to me. I saw the diary and the address book in the center of the kitchen table, and I remembered that I had to make a decision. I had to decide whether I was going to show the diary to Mr. Barrow. Whether I could give them to him would depend on whether Art might need them. I didn't think so. If they got Ed Buddy with anything, I doubted it would be the killing of Joy Lynn and the dwarf girl, Carol.

While I ate the bean with bacon soup, I read the pages Marcy had decoded. I went through them slowly, trying to gauge the effect they'd have on Mr. Barrow. I kept in front of me all I knew about him, the love and all the painful doubts he had had about her. And I tried to put myself in his place and feel the pain he'd experience when he read about Joy Lynn and Harry Falk, and all those tricks she'd turned with all those blank-faced strangers on the streets.

By the time I was chasing the last bean around the bowl, I'd reached the last entry, the one that covered the events of the day before she was killed. It had probably been written the next morning, the morning of the day she died. I got all the way through the entry, and then I stopped and went back. It jumped out at me this time.

*...He was shaking and he said the attempt to teach Ed a lesson had not worked. Some people had been hurt and he thought Ed Buddy would try to find out who had sent the men after him. He said we ought to stay put and act like we didn't know anything. I said that would be easy because I didn't know anything. He said yes I did and that I had fingered Ed Buddy for them. And if he knew he was not going to like me for that reason. But I knew better.*

I ran that around on my tongue. *But I knew better.* Why should she know better? It didn't make sense. Or did it?

I opened the diary and worked my way over to the last entry. That was it. I'd been in too much of a hurry. I'd told Marcy to decode only those entries where an Ed or an Ed Buddy were mentioned. Marcy had translated the entries for April 7 and April 12. There were four entries between those that she hadn't touched, because there'd been no Ed or Ed Buddy there. Stupid shit, dumb shit. I found a pad and a pencil and began with the entry for April 8. It took me a bit more than an hour to find what I was looking for. It was in the entry for April 11.

*...I don't know if I am doing the right thing. Maybe I have made a mistake. But I like him and he has always been nice to me and I do not want him hurt Tonight after a trick I had the john drop me at the motel and I went to his suite. He was alone and he laughed and said are you doing deliveries now? I told him I was.*

*And then I told him I had heard out on the street that some people were out to get him and they knew about the suite somehow and that was where they were going to beat him up. He wanted to know who they were and I said I had not heard any names. I could not tell him about Harry. He wanted to know when it was to happen and I said I wasn't sure but I thought it would be soon. He wanted to give me some money but I didn't feel right about that. I wouldn't take it. And he gave me a hug and thanked me. When I left the suite he was on the phone, dialing.*

*Now I am worried about Harry. Maybe I have done the wrong thing and got him in trouble. But I did not give Harry's name and there is no way he can trace it back to Harry.*

I closed the diary and pushed it away. The dumb woman had chippied on her pimp and got herself and her pimp killed. If she'd stayed out of it, she might still be alive.

I went into the bedroom and called Hump. I told him I wanted him to drop by and see some of his black pimp friends and find out two things for me, even if he had to beat it out of them with a stick.

"What's that?"

"Who organized the try on Ed Buddy. And who put the funds together and brought the two hit men in."

"You don't want much, do you?"

"You do it?"

He said he would.

Barrow came exactly at four. I heard the pickup out in the driveway and met him at the door. He looked older, pale and drained, like he'd been giving blood. He stood on my little porch and looked at the grass that needed cutting and the long hedge that needed pruning.

"You can tell me about it on the way to the jail," he said.

I shook my head. "How about some coffee? I'm expecting a call."

"You said you'd set it up so that …"

"I will," I said. "I'll put you face to face with him. That's why I'm waiting for the call."

He gave me a blank, puzzled look.

"Coffee or a beer? It's good beer weather."

He surprised me by opting for the beer.

About an hour later, Hump called. "I'm not going to be welcome around one of those bars any more."

But what he told me put the last piece in the puzzle.

# CHAPTER THIRTEEN

The hostess wanted to seat us near the low bandstand, where the girl with the long black hair that reached her waist was singing the top forty in the same voice she probably sang 1930's labor movement songs in some college coffee house a couple of years before. I shook my head at her and said we'd take a table toward the front window, the one that over looked West Peachtree.

Art and Barrow ordered beer. Hump and I told her J&B on the rocks. When she brought our orders a few minutes later, Art got out his ID and showed it to her.

"I'm expecting a call, but I don't want to be paged."

She wrote down his name on the back of a pad and carried it to the reservation clerk at the counter near the bar. Barrow leaned toward me. "Is he here?"

"Not yet." I peeled back my cuff and checked the time. It was five after eight. "Any minute now."

"I don't know if I can do it, Mr. Hardman," Barrow said.

"Sure you can." I patted him on the shoulder. "Think of it as a job of acting where you just have one line. The big thing is to give the line at the right time."

"I'll try."

"You'll do fine," I said.

I'd taken the table nearest the wall aisle. I turned my chair and watched the alcove where the elevators were. At eight-twenty-five, Wash Johnson, wearing a gray silk-blend suit and a blood-red tie, came out of the alcove and waved at the hostess. He headed for his spot at the bar. "Our boy," I said to Art.

PIMP FOR THE DEAD

Before I left the table with Art, I winked at Barrow.

The bartender placed the Bloody Mary in front of him about the time Art and I reached the bar. I tapped Wash on the shoulder and grinned at the irritation and anger that clouded his face when he saw me. "Christ, Hardman, I thought I was through with you."

Art stepped in and showed his ID. "I need to ask you a few questions."

"Oh." Wash looked at me. "Is it about Ed Buddy? I heard about it out on the street."

"About that, yes." He closed the ID case and dropped it in his coat pocket. "We've got a table."

"Sure." He scooped up his Bloody Mary and followed us the length of the room to our table. Before he sat down, while Art got another chair from an empty table nearby, he said, "I didn't mean to act that way. I really appreciate what you did."

"Appreciate your help," I said.

Hump and Wash nodded at each other. I didn't introduce Mr. Barrow. I hoped it would look like an oversight in the beginning. When we were all seated, Art said, "I think we've broken the racket."

"To the police," Wash said, lifting his Bloody Mary and sipping it.

"But we've got a few loose ends. I thought you might help us with them."

"If I can," Wash said. He was loose and easy. Then he looked across the table and saw that Barrow was staring at him, hardly blinking.

"I think we can put Buddy and his boys away, one charge or another. But it doesn't look like we can tie the killings of the two girls on him."

"Maybe it averages out," Wash said.

"My feelings, usually," Art said. "But this time, that won't wash with me. It looks now like Buddy and his friends didn't have anything to do with the deaths of Joy Lynn Barrow and the dwarf girl."

"That's crazy. Nobody else had a reason."

Barrow took that moment to lean over and whisper in my ear. It was just an act, anyway, so it didn't matter what he said. I think, through the mumble, I heard him ask how my garden was doing.

Wash saw the charade. It worried him, and he looked over at Barrow. "I don't think I got your name," he said.

Hump leaned in and cut him off. "I'm not a cop, but I've learned a few things from Hardman here. The big mistake you make sometimes with an investigation is getting locked in too early. You've got seven killings, and you want to tie all seven in a gift box and stuff them in one stud's hip pocket. Ed Buddy's, for example." He leaned back. "Maybe it's just American efficiency, not wanting to leave some of the files open."

The waitress stopped next to Art. "Phone call, Mr. Maloney."

"Excuse me." Art left the table and followed her down the aisle. Wash jerked his eyes away from Art and back to us.

"But those killings were a warning." He tapped me on the arm. "You said they were."

I shook my head. "You suggested it, Wash, and I bought it, for the time. I didn't have anything better to offer in its place."

"You got any other ideas?"

"Some," I said. "It could have been Harry Falk."

"Maybe." I could see him about ready to jump at it. He'd like for us to accept that, but he couldn't come up with a good reason to back it. "I can't see him doing it, though."

"She might have been chippying on him," I said.

"That's a bruise or two," Wash said. "Of course, there might be something we don't know about. Harry had a pretty bad temper."

"So you think it's possible?" Hump asked.

"I'd hate to think it of him, but it might be possible."

PIMP FOR THE DEAD

"And it would be neat, too." Hump reached over and got one of my smokes.

"Huh?"

"He's dead, and he can't say otherwise."

Art came back then. He was followed by the waitress with another round of drinks. "Give the ticket to Mr. Hardman," Art said.

"I wish they'd give you cops a raise," I said.

Art angled his chair so he was facing Wash. "You know what started us out on this line? The Barrow girl kept a diary. Day by day, every day."

"Is that right?" Wash lowered his eyes, away from Barrow's stare.

"Some real insights in there."

"On a hooker's life?"

"More than that. Seems she got involved. She wasn't exactly chippying with the Ed Buddy stud, but she was close. She fingered him, and then she had second thoughts and unfingered him."

"I always wondered about that girl," Wash said. "Maybe she didn't have what it takes."

"You ever do any hunting, Wash?"

"Huh?" The abrupt shift unsettled him. "Hunting? Not since I was a kid."

"You own a shotgun?"

"Me? No. I don't believe in guns."

"That's odd," Art said.

"What is?"

"The call was from a crew at your apartment. With a proper search warrant, of course. Served it on a girl who was at your place. Seems they found a pump gun in the cabinet under your sink. Another odd thing about that shotgun. It was stolen. Numbers match one stolen from a hock shop on Pryor the night before the girls were shot."

"I don't know anything about..." Wash began.

RALPH DENNIS

I reached under the table and tapped Mr. Barrow on the knee. Barrow said, "He's the one."

"What?" Art canted his head and looked at Mr. Barrow.

"He's the one. I was on the corner of Ponce de Leon and Peachtree, in front of the Georgian Terrace that night, and he was in the black Fury, and right before the light changed, he rolled down the back window. I saw the barrel of the ..."

Wash pushed back his chair and started to get to his feet. Art opened his jacket and showed him his clip holster and the butt of the .38.

"The least we can do," Art said, "is finish our drinks, since Jim there was nice enough to spring for them."

It was silent around the table. The four of us stared at Wash and sipped our drinks. After a break, the girl with the long black hair returned for another set and began with a long guitar solo that must have been designed to warn the customers that the entertainment was starting.

"It wasn't something I wanted to do," Wash said.

"Why?" Art asked.

"The hit try failed, and Buddy was shaking the town apart. The Barrow girl knew, and it was her or me. It wasn't going to be me."

I looked down at the check. A rough estimate put the total at around fifteen dollars. I got out my roll and peeled off a twenty and dropped it on the check. "Too bad about that, Wash."

"Huh?"

"It was for nothing. It was a waste. She didn't know about you, and the only way Buddy could have got to you was through her pimp, Harry Falk. And she wasn't about to finger him. She liked him too much. She might even have loved him."

I nodded at Mr. Barrow. "Ready?"

He said he was, and we walked through 590 West and out to the elevators.

168

It was dark in my driveway. A slice of light from the front door cut across the lawn. Marcy was inside, playing with the kittens while the mama cat hovered on the edges, not quite sure what she was supposed to do under the circumstances.

Barrow was behind the wheel of his pickup, and I was leaning on the window frame.

"Well, one thing I can say about you, Hardman. You did what you said you'd do."

"You helped," I said.

"Those people... people like Wash... I don't understand them."

"It's better you don't. Not many people do."

"Send me a bill," he said.

"I owe you a refund."

He shook his head. "I'm satisfied."

"The diary... do you want it when the police are through with it?"

"I don't think so. Tonight told me enough." He turned the ignition key, and what he said then was half drowned in the rush of the engine. "You should have seen her when she was four and five and six."

"I wish I'd had the chance," I said.

I stepped away from the pickup and he backed out. It was going to be a long, lonely drive back to Anson, Georgia.

❧ ❧ ❧

Art called me a couple of hours later. Marcy was out in the garage, putting the kittens back where they belonged and feeding the mama. It was the way I'd guess it. There was a pickup out on a James Benson, the pimp who'd driven the Fury for Wash.

Wash, after the failure of the try on Ed Buddy, knew he was in trouble. He guessed, as Art and I had when we'd looked over the circumstances of the shooting in the parking lot of the Executive, that Buddy had been warned. That meant Joy Lynn had done it. She was the logical one. The way he thought, it was just a matter of time before she fingered him. So he'd had the shotgun stolen, and he'd set it up with James Benson. The first time they drove by the corner that night, she hadn't been there. That was when Hump and I were taking the two girls for a ride. The second time around she'd been there with the dwarf girl, and he'd taken his chance and got off several rounds. He didn't have anything against Carol Spinks. She'd just been in the way.

"What about Harry Falk?" I asked.

"He says he didn't. That leaves Ed Buddy. Maybe Buddy thought Harry had wasted her. We might never know for sure, unless the stud you broke up decides to tell us about it."

I said I thought Bad Throat might be dumb, but I wasn't sure he was that dumb.

"We'll work on that possibility," Art said.

"What happened to Hump?"

"Last time I saw him, he was edging up on the girl singer, the one with the hair down to her ass."

"I didn't know Hump liked plastic music," I said.

Art laughed and said he'd see me and hung up. I decided I'd call Hump the next day. Late in the day, in case he convinced her his tin ear wasn't really tin.

"I have a day off tomorrow," Marcy said.

It was around midnight, and Marcy and I were out in the backyard, leaning on my terrace wall and looking over my garden. It was impressive, the slightly uneven rows where I'd planted the corn, the Chinese cabbage and the butter beans, and the humps where the hills of summer and zucchini squash were. So far, the only things above ground were the tomato plants, and they looked like they'd grown an inch or two in the last couple of days.

In the distance, there was a thin, wiggle of lightning.

"Those damned Chinese cabbages aren't doing anything. I think they're growing downward."

"I thought we might pack a picnic lunch and drive up to Stone Mountain," she said.

"Toward China," I said.

There was another pale slice of lightning, this time closer, and a light rain began to fall.

The mama cat walked the terrace wall. She paused at Marcy's gin and tonic and sniffed it, then stepped over it.

"Listen to those seeds opening," I said.

Marcy came over and fitted herself into the hollow of my shoulder, and I blew into her ear, and the mama cat left us and crapped on one of the hills where the zucchini seeds were.

# AFTERWORD

## A Hardman is Good to Find
## By Paul Bishop

In 1974, *Atlanta Deathwatch*, the first Hardman novel by Ralph Dennis, debuted as a paperback original from Popular Library. It was done an immediate and deliberate disservice by its publisher, who packaged the book as a low rent rip-off of *The Executioner* and the other men's adventure paperback series that were popular at the time. It was branded *Hardman #1* and given a crappy cover in keeping with the standard men's adventure genre artwork established by Pinnacle, Manor Books, Zebra and other paperback original publishers (while this is true, there is something so bad about the original covers that they have become retro-cool and collectable).

But the *Hardman* series was different. It was closer in quality, tone, and style to Ed McBain's 87$^{th}$ *Precinct* books. It had little in common with *The Destroyer*, *The Penetrator*, and other paperback vigilantes. Hardman's closest contemporary was the hardboiled cop series *Razoni & Jackson* written by Warren Murphy (and the acknowledged inspiration for the *Lethal Weapon* films).

Hardman is a tough guy, but he's also middle-aged, overweight, out of shape, and on occasion not too smart. As readers, we know there is no way we could be *The Executioner*, but we could be Hardman.

So why were the *Hardman* books packaged like *The Executioner* when it clearly wasn't? To find the answer, we have to look at the *Hardman* books in the context of their time. And to do that, I'm going to have to drag you down a rabbit hole with me.

Here we go …

Film and fiction have always reflected the cultural issues of the time in which they were produced. They are the pop culture prism through which we examine societal concerns. We use the images on screens and the text on pages to try out solutions, discard them, and try on another—like a bride searching for the perfect wedding dress. And like the bride, we sometimes have to settle for something that doesn't make our butts look fat.

Being the redheaded stepchild of decades, the '70s is a perfect example of how this works. On the losing end of an unpopular war, the '70s was a dope-fueled mashup of political angst and discordant impossibilities, like peace, man. Not as original as the '60s, and not as cool as the '80s (when TV cops wore pastel colors and Italian loafers without socks), the '70s were a generational placeholder.

The decade did offer a few scattered gems. There were no safe zones, cuddling clubs, or human flesh-bags looking for any reason to be offended or get mentioned on TMZ. You could eat beef and drink soda. Real men jogged. David Bowie released Diamond Dogs. Pineapple upside-down cake was a thing. And the Sex Pistols were dropped six days after signing with A&M records for being too outrageous to be kept on a leash.

But the dark side of the '70s outweighed even pineapple upside-down cake. Sacrificed on the altar of politics and war-mongering, hardened veterans returned to the Land of the Free with shrapnel scars, bullet wounds, missing limbs, thousand yard stares, and haunting memories of their many brothers who died violently in an inhospitable Asian jungle.

They expected a hero's welcome, or at least, a display of gratitude. What they got was the chilling confusion of being scapegoated as baby killers. While they had been fighting and dying, the '70s had been decoupaged with torn photos of disco, bell bottoms, leg warmers, leisure suits for men, and peace signs. Ten years after Timothy Leary chanted, turn on, tune in, and drop out, his mid-'60s rallying cry had become a reality for the directionless '70s.

To rescue the decade from the Pit of Ennui, heroes were needed—heroes of the people, created by the people, for the people. As it had in another generation, film and fiction rose as Spartans to give us a testing zone where we could attempt to understand our turmoil, our angers, and our inadequacies.

To understand this phenomenon, we must digress to the end of another war. Like the '70s Viet Nam era vets, American fighting men coming home from WWII also had trouble fitting back into a society they didn't recognize.

Post World War II America was supposed to revert to the idyllic values of the traditional family. Rosie the Riveter would willingly give her job back to a man, get out of the factory, put on an apron, and go back into the kitchen. Men would come back from the war unfazed by their experiences to take up the responsibility of providing for their families without missing a beat. If the American family was not restored to the pinnacle of its idealized, mythological form, how could we justify everything we sacrificed while fighting for our freedom and the freedom of our allies?

However, much of America wasn't buying it. We had been to the gates of Hell and beyond. We were warriors, and supporters of warriors. We had discovered our dark sides where we were selfish, driven, ambitious, strategic, and most importantly, we had discovered we were killers. To win a war on the largest scale imaginable, we had to go dark, black even, embracing the human wildness within.

But with peace came the expectation of normal. Everywhere we turned, we were being press-ganged into rigid conformity.

Television, Madison Avenue, the stress of keeping up appearances, the responsibility for too many decisions in a world without orders to follow, created a human pressure cooker. There had to be an outlet for our wildness, our darkness, our pent up adrenaline, a way to understand the horror we had been through.

Movies gave us a conduit as *film noir* invaded cinemas everywhere. The genre pierced the pustules of our pain because the characters on the screen were visibly broken and jagged—they showed on the outside what we were feeling inside.

Film noir characters were desperate individuals gladly paving their own road to Hell rather than surrender to a lobotomized life in suburbia. There was something wrong with them, something the false sheen of domesticated bliss could not fix. War had released our demons and there was no stuffing them back in the jar.

Americans knew they were supposed to want things bright and shiny, yet they flocked in droves to the movie theaters to see the dark seamy sides of life. During the war, they had lived film noir and knew it felt cool to be legitimately bad. Film noir was a drug, and the cinematic justifications of our feelings could not be produced fast enough to keep up with demand.

The follow-up to film noir's punch to the mouth of conformity, was that bastard of genre fiction, the Men's Adventure Magazines. During their heydays from the '40s through the '50s, these slick-cover magazines catered to males with lurid true tales of adventure, of true wartime daring, exotic travel, and true attacks by wild animals of every ilk—as in Weasels Ripped My Flesh.

Most of the covers on the men's adventure magazines featured scantily clad, tiny-waisted, big breasted women being rescued from peril by muscular male heroes toting big guns, spears, knives, and other phallic symbols. The covers also featured these same beautiful women about to be whipped, burned, fed to alligators, or sold into sexual slavery by leering Nazi officers, evil

Nazi doctors, and horrendous Nazi torturers—who would eventually morph into outlaw bikers with the same twisted desires.

There was a need within us to confront such perversions—for men to know there was still a battle they could fight, still a damsel they could rescue (as they had rescued their wives, girlfriends, and families through the hell of battle). They needed a way to be an unquestioned hero, to forge an explanation for the terrors and revulsions heaped upon them in war. To feel something—anything—again.

Tawdry and salacious enough to be hidden down the sides of dad's armchair or stacked in a dark corner of his garage, the men's adventure magazines were a safe escape for men craving an existence beyond the world being forced upon, a world of societal expectations, disapproval, and repression.

Film and fiction provided a method to confront our fears by proxy until real solutions could catch up with society. When the public psyche was ready to move on, film noir and men's adventure magazines disappeared from the mainstream, their mission accomplished.

Fast forward to the '70s. Wars it appeared were not restricted to foreign soils. There was a war going on at home...a war on crime. A war we were losing—again. Our enemies were legion: Street criminals; shifty defense lawyers equipped with briefcases full of technicalities; delinquency; political and institutional corruption; the scourge of drugs; and the resurgence of organized crime—the Mafia; the Mob; the Felons of Oz—hiding behind their vast criminal empire.

After Viet Nam, we were confused, angry, and disoriented. We wanted a stiff drink and a way to jump off the spinning teacups. We needed a cause to unite us. Casting about, the tattered American spirit latched on to the war on crime, naïvely believing it was a war we could win. However, we needed somebody to show us how to fight this new battle, so we resurrected our old warriors—film and fiction—dressed them in new armor and sent them into the fray.

Film struck the first blow. Its weapons were language, adult content, sexuality, and violence—all on the big screen. The loosening of restrictions on these cinematic elements reflected the counter-culture's embrace of free love, edgy rock-n-roll, the civil rights movement, changing gender roles and drug use. Old style Hollywood moguls were dying out and a new generation of film makers was eager to take their place. Hollywood was stretching conventional boundaries as films began to aggressively expose the dark underbelly of the times.

Fiction joined the battle bringing a game changing big gun, the ultimate in '70s darkness... *Death Wish.*

Brian Garfield's 1972 novel, and the subsequent 1974 film starring Charles Bronson, spoke to the '70s as nothing else could. It addressed the heart of our frustration. But *Death Wish* was a sheep in wolf's clothing. It was a be-careful-what-you-wish-for warning hidden (perhaps too well) beneath a savage fable of wish fulfillment and revenge.

Caught between literary and genre fiction, *Death Wish* destroyed the ramparts of convention and loosed the dogs of war. Led by Don Pendleton, dirty dozens of hard-bitten, cynical, fast typing genre writers charged into the breech. With his novel, *The Executioner #1: The War Against the Mafia*, Pendleton spawned a whole new fiction genre of men's adventure paperback original series.

The Executioner Mack Bolan's deadly fighting skills and fearsome reputation were forged in the hell of Viet Nam. When he returned stateside to find his family destroyed by drugs and criminals, Bolan geared up to bring the hell of war down on the Medusa head of organized crime.

The men's adventure paperback series of the '70s were akin to the men's adventure magazines of the '50s, but there was one big difference. The true stories in the men's adventure magazines of the '50s looked (albeit salaciously) to past events. But the men's adventure paperback series of the '70s looked to the present and to the future beyond.

The simple, yet spiritually patriotic theme, as established by Pendleton, of taking back the streets of America from pimps and mobsters, unleashed the imagination of a new generation of pulp writers. Uncountable men's adventure paperback series exploded onto spinner racks in every five-&-dime, supermarket, and drugstore across the country. Clearly, the American psyche was willing to accept the war on crime could only be won by lone vigilantes rising up from the ranks of the everyman to massacre robbers, thieves, drug lords, corrupt cops, pimps, hitmen, hoods, goons, lowlifes and Mafia dons across the country.

The reading public's appetite for the genre appeared insatiable. *The Executioner, The Destroyer, The Penetrator, The Expeditor, The Inquisitor, The Liquidator,* and *the Protector* joined the likes of *The Death Merchant, The Revenger, The Killmaster, The Marksman, The Sharpshooter,* and dozens of other mercenaries, reformed hitmen, and *Death Wish*-lite vigilantes to fight our battle.

The men's adventure paperback series quickly established a set of clichés—Sexy large breasted women are in need of rescue everywhere. Unlimited ammunition is always available. A knife thrown by a hero at any range is instantly fatal. For supposedly being a secret art, ninjas proliferate like SDTs. The faithful, yet weak and desperate companion always saves the hero's ass in a pinch. Explosives always go off in the nick of time. Before killing the captured hero, super villains will always explain their nefarious plot, giving the hero the chance to escape. The key to victory is courage and smart-ass remarks.

In mainstream fiction, when all is said and done, a great deal is said and very little done. In genre fiction, not much is said, but a great deal is done, which finally gets us to the bottom of the rabbit hole and to the tea party with Hardman and Hump.

The men's adventure paperback series' bred many similarly packaged series, each a slightly blurry version of the original mold. Other genres, Westerns in particular, sought to tart up their own genre's standard tropes by dressing them up as men's adventure series.

The *Hardman* series brought its own hyper-realistic take to the war on crime. It was new. It was brilliant. It was different.

Unfortunately, it was bought by Popular Library, which built their publishing business on knock-offs of whatever was hot at the time. Popular Library did not establish trends. Instead, they chased them, picking up the leftover genre dollars along the way.

Faced with the superior writing quality of the *Hardman* books, Popular Library panicked. They recognized the series was a hybrid, but they didn't trust it to find its own niche in the market. Popular Library didn't trust different.

Having no clue how to sell different, the publisher threw Hardman overboard to flounder in the vast sea of vigilantes and *Death Wish* imitators.

As the '70s took hold of its destiny, the men's adventure series paperbacks fell out of favor. Some held on through the '80s, but eventually they too disappeared the same way film noir and men's adventure magazines did when their cultural stress release was no longer needed.

By touting the *Hardman* series as something it wasn't, the books got short shrift and quickly fell into the same obscurity as the men's adventure genre. Hardman deserved much better.

Even in obscurity, the *Hardman* books continue to be something special. While the lingo and attitudes were warts of the '70s, the characters, their relationships, and the quality of Dennis' writing was timeless. The series became a hidden genre gem. It was whispered about only by the most hardcore genre fans—who turned collecting the twelve sacred Hardman books into a quest of mythical proportions.

However, it appears you can't keep a Hardman down. Once Brash Books co-founder Lee Goldberg discovered *Hardman*, he began a legendary quest of his own to bring the series back into the mainstream. And now he has succeeded with the publication of these new editions. Wrapped in stunning and appropriate covers, this lost literary treasure of the '70s is finally getting the recognition it deserves, and Jim Hardman and Hump Evans have found themselves officially added to the pantheon of hardboiled greats.

*Paul Bishop is a 35-year veteran of the Los Angeles Police Department. His career included a three year tour with his department's Anti-Terrorist Division and over twenty-five years' experience in the investigation of sex crimes. Twice honored as LAPD's Detective of the Year, Paul also received the Quality and Productivity Commission Award from the City of Los Angeles. He currently conducts law enforcement related seminars for city, state, and private agencies.*

*Paul is the author of fifteen novels and has written numerous scripts for episodic television and feature films. His latest book, Lie Catchers, is the first in a new series featuring top LAPD interrogators Ray Pagan and Calamity Jane Randall.*

# ABOUT THE AUTHOR

Ralph Dennis isn't a household name... but he should be. He is widely considered among crime writers as a master of the genre, denied the recognition he deserved because his twelve *Hardman* books, which are beloved and highly sought-after collectables now, were poorly packaged in the 1970s by Popular Library as a cheap men's action-adventure paperbacks with numbered titles.

Even so, some top critics saw past the cheesy covers and noticed that he was producing work as good as John D. MacDonald, Raymond Chandler, Chester Himes, Dashiell Hammett, and Ross MacDonald.

The *New York Times* praised the *Hardman* novels for "expert writing, plotting, and an unusual degree of sensitivity. Dennis has mastered the genre and supplied top entertainment." The *Philadelphia Daily News* proclaimed *Hardman* "the best series around, but they've got such terrible covers..."

Unfortunately, Popular Library didn't take the hint and continued to present the series like hack work, dooming the novels to a short shelf-life and obscurity... except among generations of crime writers, like novelist Joe R. Lansdale (the *Hap & Leonard* series) and screenwriter Shane Black (the *Lethal Weapon* movies), who've kept Dennis' legacy alive through word-of-mouth and by acknowledging his influence on their stellar work.

Ralph Dennis wrote three other novels that were published outside of the *Hardman* series—*Atlanta, Deadman's Game* and

*MacTaggart's War*—but he wasn't able to reach the wide audience, or gain the critical acclaim, that he deserved during his lifetime.

He was born in 1931 in Sumter, South Carolina, and received a masters degree from University of North Carolina, where he later taught film and television writing after serving a stint in the Navy. At the time of his death in 1988, he was working at a bookstore in Atlanta and had a file cabinet full of unpublished novels.

Brash Books will be releasing the entire *Hardman* series, his three other published novels, and his long-lost manuscripts.

65632049R00114